A Gentleman of Leisure

Edgar Fawcett

Contents

A Gentleman
of Leisure

BY

Edgar Fawcett

A GENTLEMAN OF LEISURE.

I.

ONE agreeable winter morning, while the grim roar of painted omnibuses rose from Broadway between two brisk streams of moving humanity, a gentleman named Mr. Townsend Spring suddenly stopped under the big, gray, many-windowed structure of the New Post-Office, and held out his hand to another gentleman, who was passing him unnoticed.

"Bless my soul, Wainwright! said Mr. Spring. "What are *you* doing in a place like New York?"

"I thought I would come over and look about a little," said the gentleman thus addressed.

This latter speaker was, perhaps, in his twenty-sixth year. e was of middle height and compact build; he was extremely blond; the moustache shading his serious mouth was even a shade lighter than his light hair. His features were all strong and regular, but each was so stamped with gravity and composure that you somehow thought of him as a person eminently quiet and reputable before you observed that he was also handsome. His eyes were blue and calm, and their clearness of coloring sometimes gave the impression of coldness besides. He was dressed with the peculiar grace of all well-attired Englishmen, which is another way of saying that his clothes fitted him faultlessly and yet looked as if they had received only the most transient attention on the part of their wearer. Mr. Clinton Wainwright was not an Englishman; but to record this fact is like casually mentioning the foreign origin of some vegetable growth which we have seen for years prosperously domesticated. He had lived a long time in England, though American by birth. His sympathies, as the phrase goes, were entirely with the mother country. Affairs relating to a large inheritance from a deceased kinsman had brought him across the ocean. He meant that his sojourn here should not exceed three months at the most. He expected to be a little amused and a great deal bored by the trip, but the financial reasons why he should take it had of late grown imperative. It cost him an effort, however, to go at all. He had not realized, until the hour came for starting, how his dislike of things transatlantic had gradually struck deeper roots as years went on. This morning, when his meeting with Mr. Townsend Spring occurred, it was scarcely two days since he had quitted the steamer. He said as much to his companion, who at once responded,—

"I suppose you've been busy, thus far, in looking up your relations.

"Oh, no," replied Wainwright. "Except a fourth cousin or two, I have no relations left. Our direct line, as one might say, threatens to become extinct with myself."

"By Jove, I hope not," said Spring, with a full laugh. Then he shook his head, and added, "I'm sure there isn't much chance of that. The way you noticed all the pretty girls last summer in Switzerland meant that you d never die a bachelor. And I don't forget, either, how some of the pretty girls noticed you."

"You're very good, really," said Wainwright. He spoke, as he always spoke, with what we call a broad accent, but there was now the least hint of a sarcastic drawl in his tones. He thrust a hand into each vertical side-pocket of his loose trousers, till the scant front of his cutaway morning coat gave the effect of a skirtless jacket. He stared at Spring with a sort of blank mildness. He considered him quite a dreadful creature. Last summer he had interfered most jarringly with the poetry of the Alps and glaciers, but now he seemed in good harmony with the raw smartness of an American thoroughfare. Wainwright had known a fellow something like him, who had been in his own year at Oxford. True, the refinements of association had smoothed away some of his co-disciple's barbarisms. But Spring stood forth at all times in bald, immoderate crudity.

"It's lucky I came across you," now said Mr. Spring, with fine consciousness that he was deepening a past favorable opinion. "I'll put you down at the Metropolitan Club. It's the biggest and finest club in the country; it's up to anything you've got in England, *I* think.

"Ah?" said Wainwright, whose satire was sometimes stealthy, but never uncivil, and whose good breeding was known by his friends to have survived every sort of social test. It must be a very fine club."

"Yes, indeed," rattled on Spring. "I know you'll say so, too, when you've seen the Metropolitan." He was a man not over two and thirty. He had a thick-set figure and a bluff, florid face, with that bluish tinge about either plump cheek which is said to denote vinous dinners and late revels. But his small eyes twinkled freshly, and his frame and movements bespoke an unimpaired fund of health. He had an immense lemon-colored mustache, that quite hid his mouth, making two bulging ovals on each side of it, where the coarse, glossy hairs met in a curved point at either end. His dress was modish, with a dapper dandyism in the make and pattern of its vivid plaids. He wore a cravat of crimson satin, sprinkled with large white sprays, like wallpaper, and pierced with a scarf-pin that was a jockey's cap and riding-whip joined together in a sort of golden arabesque. "But I'm going to do more for you than put you down there at the club," Mr. Spring now continued. "I'm going to make you come and see my wife."

"I shall be most happy to come," said Wainwright, wren prompt courtesy.

"There's a good deal going on just now," proceeded his companion. "We can make things rather jolly for you, if you want; we can show you about. Fanny hasn't forgotten you; she still talks of you every now and then; she was always death on you English chaps. . . . . Hold up a second; I'll give you a card. Here it is, ... No.——West Thirty-Fifth Street. You can pop in on us whenever you please." Mr. Spring here produced an ornate wallet of Russian leather, bearing a gilt monogram of his initials. Then, after giving Wainwright the card, he added, "You'll excuse me, old fellow, if I hurry right off. The Street's in a kind of flurry to-day, and I've got to keep my wits about me. Ever so glad to have met you. Don't forget, now, to give us a call as soon as you can manage."

Away darted Mr. Spring, leaving his hearer quite willing to agree with him that the street was in a remarkable flurry. Wainwright did not perceive the usual idiomatic allusion to Wall Street, although vaguely aware that Townsend Spring was a stock-broker. An extraordinary violence and confusion seemed reigning in Broadway. The liveliest bustle of London thoroughfares did not surpass it. He had just come from his banker, and he was now returning to his hotel. During the long walk that followed, Wainwright decided that he would call upon Mrs. Spring. He could not go that evening, for he was engaged to dine with his banker; but he would go, nevertheless, hereafter. He had liked Mrs. Spring in Switzerland. She had been the first American lady to whom he had ever felt attracted; indeed, she had been the first whose acquaintance he had ever cared to seek. Till now, he had believed her delightfully exceptional among per countrywomen, but of late this impression had changed; he began to realize the importance of his mistake. As he now passed along Fifth Avenue, noting the brown-stone prosperity of its high-stooped mansions, the glimpses of sumptuous drapery at the plate-glass windows, the occasional porcelain jardinière or costly bit of bronze, that suggested richer luxuries lying beyond them, he was also sensible of a similar surprise regarding many of the ladies whom he met. He found himself perpetually reminded of Mrs. Spring, and perpetually made to feel that he was a very long distance away from London. He had never been to Paris; his Swiss trip had been his only experience of the Continent; he was about as "insular" a person as twenty youthful years of residence in England are commonly able to produce. For this reason, the feminine figures that now passed him seemed often distinguished by a delicacy and elegance mat appealed with fascinating novelty to ms sense of beauty and refinement. It is safe to say that Wainwright had expected uncouth-ness and vulgarity everywhere. It must be old of him at once, as a matter of pure justice, that he had arrived in New York with the feelings neither of a snob nor a prig; that he was the sort of young gentleman who must fairly and honestly earn the title of a very good fellow, no matter in what circle of society fate should cast him; but that he had taken the tint of certain surrounding beliefs as naturally as water reflects sky. He bad had no doubts whatever on the subject of America being as small nationally as it was large geographically. He had moved among a set of English people who very rarely take the trouble even to sneer at this country; they were of the sort who remember only incidentally that this is the place the Cunard steamers make for when not sailing eastward. They belonged distinctly to the aristocracy. Wainwright's mother, who had died while he was at Oxford, had married a second time in England, and the young man's step-father had been nearly related to an earl. Wainwright had been accepted at patrician firesides without a single fastidious murmur. His American birth was almost ignored, or at best remembered against him with lenient grace, like the peccadilloes of some deceased kinsman.

He dressed himself for the dinner with his banker, this evening, in a good deal of curious expectancy. He had had several sharp surprises already, and he was now prepared for several more. The banker himself, Mr. Bodenstein, had seemed to him a very charming gentleman. Mr. Bodenstein was of German birth; he spoke English with a slight accent. He was extremely bald, had bright-red side-whiskers, a fat, shapeless nose, and thick, loose lips. But his double-breasted coat was of speckless broadcloth and perfect fit; he carried gold eye-glasses, which he would sometimes wave gracefully while speaking. He could talk with sound sense on numberless subjects; he was famous as a shrewd financier, and owned a superb gallery of paintings; he had one palatial home on Fifth Avenue and another at Newport; he was a member of the Jockey Club, and an enthusiastic patron of the turf. He had no library worth the name, but he read men and newspapers instead, and both with careful thoroughness. He had greatly bettered himself, in a social sense, some fifteen years ago, by marrying a beautiful and charming lady, of fine Knickerbocker lineage. His wealth was enormous, and his hospitalities were princely.

The hour at which he had asked Wainwright to dine with him was seven o'clock. Our young Anglo-American felt a lively thrill of surprise on hearing that anybody in his native country dined at seven. He had supposed two in the afternoon to be a much more probable hour.

II.

WAINWRIGHT had himself driven in a cab from his hotel to Mr. Bodenstein's Fifth Avenue mansion. One butler opened the door for him; another removed his wraps, with skillful expedition. The young man was then ushered from a hall of noble proportions into a suite of drawing-rooms, grander still. Everywhere gleamed quiet splendor of ornamentation, ruled by the most discreet taste. Mr. Bodenstein, looking uglier, but quite as gentlemanly, in his snowy neck-tie and faultless evening dress, came forward with outstretched hand. He at once presented Wainwright to his wife. Mrs. Bodenstein was young, blonde, and beautiful. She wore a dress of sky-blue velvet, cut high in the neck, and studded with buttons, each of which was a large diamond. She had a frill of fluted lace about her throat, from which her delicate head seemed to break forth like a flower. She struck Wainwright as a most enchanting person. He had ceased to be merely surprised; he was bewildered. It seemed to him at this moment as if he could not possibly be in New York. While Mrs. Bodenstein was uttering sentences to him that meant nothing but were spoken with a most bewitching ease and grace, Wainwright observed that here and there about the room were seated ladies and gentlemen whose postures and costumes bore a distinctive elegance. In his rapid eye-sweep, he saw a slim girl with a robe of vapory rose-color, and a face like tinted porcelain; she was talking to a gentleman whose expansive shirt-bosom and lustrous, pointed shoes gave him the air of somebody who might have lounged about a select London club. Poor Wainwright could not understand matters at all. This was, somehow, not America. He had come prepared to be astonished, but in a radically different way.

"I think everybody is here," Mrs. Bodenstein presently said to him. She had a dimple in either cheek, which waited upon her frequent smiles with a delicious punctuality. She now smiled her very brightest, and the dimples looked like two deep little creases in two rose leaves. "I shall ask you to go in with me," she proceeded, and slipped her hand into Wainwright's arm. He felt instantly that he was the honored guest of the evening. They moved toward the dining-room together, and a rustling tram of followers promptly succeeded them. Wainwright soon found himself seated at Mrs. Bodenstein's right, before a table that glittered with glass and silver, and bore in its centre a superb flowery embellishment. On his left sat a young girl, to whom Mrs. Bodenstein presented him, while the oysters were being eaten and the white wine was being poured. "This is my cousin, Miss Spuytenduyvil," said Mrs. Bodenstein, with gentle sociality, "and I am sure that you will get on very nicely together.

Wainwright looked at his new acquaintance, and asked himself what grounds her appearance presented for their future harmonious intercourse. Miss Spuytenduyvil had a pale, narrow face, with small, dim eyes, over which the lids would sometimes droop in almost somnolent languor. But her companion soon found that she was neither sleepy nor indifferent. A strong interest for fresh observation and discovery had of late sprung up within Wainwright. It was a feeling whose growth could be marked by hours; it had been developed through a series of mild shocks.

He had found himself suddenly transformed from a sort of dispassionate pilgrim into a note-maker of vigilant zeal. He could ill account for the change; he had a faint sense of its being only half resultant from mere piqued curiosity; there seemed a furtive warmth behind it, whose just measure and origin he was destined afterward to gauge and value. It was not yet time for Wainwright to discover that he could do anything so unforeseen as to feel fondly toward the country of his birth.

Miss Spuytenduyvil had a thin, rather harsh voice, which aptly suited the occasional wintry flicker of her smile. Wainwright found him-self watching her with studious intentness. He had formed an idea that she might be typical and representative after some peculiar fashion, but he was already in much doubt as to whether she would be agreeably so.

"I suppose you have met very few American ladies, said Miss Spuytenduyvil, opening conversation.

I had met only one, replied Wainwright, "before coming to tins country."

Miss Spuytenduyvil was about to touch a glass of ice-water to her pale, cold lips. But she set down the goblet before doing so, and asked with direct emphasis,—

"And pray who was she? A New York lady?"

"Yes," said Wainwright. "Her name is Mrs. Townsend Spring. Do you know her?"

"Oh, no," replied the young girl. She now drank her ice-water. Then she fastened a little clinking bracelet on one of her spare, white arms. "I know whom you mean, however."

"I think her very nice," said Wainwright. "I'm sure you would, too, if you knew her."

Miss Spuytenduyvil gave a chilly little rattle of laughter. "There is very small chance of my knowing her, she said, with prim crisp-ness. Then she bent her putted and ringleted head quite low over a raw oyster.

Wainwright wondered if he had stumbled upon any awkward family quarrel. "Good gracious!" he said, "I hope you don't mean that Mrs. Spring is some cousin with whom you have had a falling out. That would be a most unlucky mishap for me, truly!

His companion gave a start, and looked at him with a very shocked expression. "Cousin!" she repeated, and threw back her head with another faint, mirthless laugh. Wainwright thought he had seldom seen a more unpleasantly arrogant look. "I merely meant, explained Miss Spuytenduyvil, "that the lady whom you mentioned is not in my set."

"Oh," said Wainwright. A light had begun to break upon him. He perceived that this young lady was indeed a typical person. But her type struck him, just at this moment, as the most alarmingly unexpected thing he could possibly have encountered. "Pray tell me," he continued, in the voice of one who puts a most serious question, "what does your last phrase mean? I assure you, I ask purely for information."

Miss Spuytenduyvil had lost her haughty demeanor. She leaned quite affably toward Wainwright; he saw, now, that her eyes were of a slaty, opaque hue, with only a speck of dull light in each. She was smiling, and he concluded that he did not like her smile any better than her laugh.

"I forgot," she said, "how ignorant you English people are about everything American."

"But I am an American," said Wainwright.

"Oh, true. Yet you have lived so long in England. I meant that this Mrs. Spring is taken up by a few of the best people, but then.... how shall I say it?.... well, she is nobody at all."

"I thought her decidedly somebody," objected Wainwright, with mild humor.

"Oh, she is loud enough; she makes herself felt. She came from the country, somewhere. It is dreadful to see that sort of person getting about everywhere." Here Miss Spuytenduyvil shrugged her slim shoulders. "Really," she went on, "you compel me to be very explicit. Not that I object to being explicit in these matters. It isn't thought good taste, I know. But then I am very indignant against our modern society."

"I am glad that you take pity on the ignorance of a fellow countryman," said Wainwright, with artful humility. He had secretly made up his mind that Miss Spuytenduyvil was one of the most disagreeable young person he had ever met.

"Are you so very ignorant of all American ways?" she asked, with one of her smiles, that had in it the hardness of a penknife-blade.

"I am afraid that I am, he laughed.

"But you surely supposed that we had grades of society here."

Wainwright was silent for a moment. "I confess," he presently said, "that I had not given the subject any thought whatever."

Miss Spuytenduyvil took the least sip of her white wine. She had begun to look sarcastically amused. "Then you want me to go on explaining?" she said.

"If you will be so kind."

A gentle hum of talk had now risen on all sides; the air was tenderly fragrant with the scent of tea-rose and violet. Wainwright let his eyes wander over the broad table, and assured himself that no feast could have been ordered with more quiet magnificence; he looked at the row of rich-clad ladies, some lovely as were the roses themselves; he marked the noiseless attendants glide over the soft carpets. He lifted his gaze, and saw an arras of crimson velvet drooping from a gilt rod, like the tapestries in pictures of old castle-chambers; not far away was a deep alcove-window, whose panes were colored with mediaeval effect, and here a tropic plant reared from the dimness its huge, dark, glossy fans. Overhead, the ceiling was crossed and corniced with massive lines of mellow-toned Gothic woodwork. Wainwright silently wondered. Here, in a republican land, he found himself confronted by traits of the most aristocratic significance. And Miss Spuytenduyvil, with her finical daintiness, her mincing artificiality, well suited these undemocratic surroundings. Wainwright had a fancy, as he watched her, that with some changes of language and costume she had existed a century or so before, among the high-shoed and powdered ladies who aired their brocades at Bourbon courts.

Her next words were measured and deliberative. "It is a very hard matter to explain,' she said. "People don't usually talk about it at all. One usually passes over the whole subject. That is thought to be the wisest plan. I regret to tell you, Mr. Wainwright, that those who should take the most pains to keep our best society in a select state are often the most careless about doing so. New people are buying their way in every year, every month. It's very sad, but it's true."

"But what should make it the best society? asked Wainwright.

Miss Spuytenduyvil looked slightly peevish. "Dear me, what makes anything any thing, Mr. Wainwright?

"Oh, now you are plunging into generalities. I am afraid you are not a very patient expositor. Or am I too unmatured a pupil? What I meant was"—

"Oh, I know what you meant," interrupted the young lady, with quiet sharpness. "You wanted to know whether wealth does not decide everything with us. But I assure you it **ought** not to do so. Of course there might be exceptional cases, just as there are in England. But here, as there, the chief qualification for moving in high circles should be to have good birth."

Wainwright looked very puzzled. "But everybody here is supposed to be born alike," he said.

"Supposed to be!" echoed his companion, with an accent of satire on the first word. Miss Spuytenduyvil now turned her sedate face full upon her neighbor. She had heightened her lean shoulders a little, and was bending toward Wainwright with an expression which made him feel how important she considered that her next remark must prove. "Pray let me ask **you** a question," she said.

"Oh, willingly."

"Why do you think that Mr. Bodenstein requested you to dine with him to-day?"

Wainwright reflected for a moment. "Upon my word," he said, "I know only one reason: I had selected him as my banker."

"As if that were any reason!" softly exclaimed Miss Spuytenduyvil.

"I have not the remotest idea of any other. If there is another, I wish you would enlighten me concerning it."

"Enlighten you! Why, good gracious! you **must** know that you are a Wainwright!"

"I have generally been under that impression."

"Oh, pshaw, you don't understand! I mean one of **the** Wainwrights. Everybody knows your family, here."

"But I haven't any family. They are all dead."

"That doesn't make the slightest difference. They are remembered; they were among oar leading people; they. . . . how shall I put it? You want one to be so dreadfully exact. Do you know, we are distantly related to each other?

"I had not an idea of it."

"Oh, yes. A Wainwright once married a Spuytenduyvil. You help to make a branch our genealogical tree."

"I am very glad to have rendered you any such material assistance. Is that why Mr. Bodenstein invited me here to-night?"

"Oh, no. You have a genealogical tree of your own."

"Is it possible? said Wainwright, with a momentary smile of keen amusement. "I was unprepared to find any such species of vegetation on these shores. It's a very different thing from the primeval hemlock that Long-fellow tells us about, isn't it?

"Oh, now you are sneering at this country. Well, you will be in the fashion there. So many people do it." Here Miss Spuytenduyvil straightened herself, with an air of almost forbidding severity. "For my part, I **never** do it. I am too proud of having ancestors who have helped to make the country what it is."

This struck Wainwright as a rather clever speech. He had just begun to wonder whether his companion had not an undercurrent of real shrewdness hidden beneath her fanatical gentility. But at this moment Mrs. Bodenstein, seated, as we know, on his other side, claimed his attention by one of those remarks which may reach us clad in such facile expression as to win our lenient disregard of their being platitudes. Wainwright soon discovered that his hostess was, in her way, a mistress of platitude. He found, after a long talk with this lady, that her command of commonplace amounted to a distinct talent. She was delightful to watch, with her ideal complexion, her sweet, liquid eyes, and her phenomenal dimples. But when you had separated what she said from her winsome, mellifluous manner of saying it, you felt that the division brought about a pitiable result. It was quite impossible to define her except in negatives; after you had concluded that she was low-voiced, of faultless breeding and exceptionally handsome, there seemed to remain an incalculable number of things that she was not. Miss Spuytenduyvil became glaringly characteristic when contrasted with her. The latter was sitting quite silent and unoccupied, when Wainwright again turned toward her, after his long resultless talk with Mrs. Bodenstein had ended. She looked colder and more self-poised than ever. She had a little block of Neapolitan ice before her, but she had eaten only the white portion of it, leaving the remainder to melt away in pink and green ruin on her enameled plate. It struck Wainwright that she might, perhaps, have eschewed these vivid colors as representing too warm a species of diet for her curiously frigid temperament. While the odd fancy brought a smile to his lips—and a smile was rather rare with him, though it always threw a sparkle up into his quiet blue eyes when it came—Miss Spuytenduyvil addressed him in her slow, clean-cut way.

"You have been having a very long talk with my cousin," she said. "What have you been talking about?"

"I really can't tell you," answered Wainwright, after a brief pause.

"Oh," said Miss Spuytenduyvil, with rigid demureness, "then you have not been getting any new information? I suppose you think my cousin charming; everybody does. She was a great success before she became Mrs. Bodenstein."

"And is that title a guarantee for still greater success?" asked Wainwright, who found himself naturally dropping into the interrogative again, before this placid, matter-of-fact curtness that once more assailed him.

Miss Spuytenduyvil made a long, slow nod, that was, somehow, like a fiat. "Of course," she said. "My cousin was a Miss Amsterdam." Then she gave one of her laughs, that sounded to Wainwright as though there was the click of dice in it. "Truly, it seems so odd for any one not to know about these things. Mr. Bodenstein is a perfect gentleman, and immensely wealthy. It was considered a very fine match for Kate. I was quite a little girl then. I remember that I disapproved of it. But I have since become reconciled."

"Oh, that is very fortunate," said Wainwright, with a certain non-committal amiability that may or may not have sheathed considerable irony. He had a droll, momentary vision of a little pale-faced Miss Spuytenduyvil, in short frocks, with budding theories about her valuable Dutch birth.

"I hope you have enjoyed your conversation with my cousin, said the young lady, breaking, a rather long silence.

"Oh, yes, very much," replied Wainwright, who knew of nothing less ordinary to say.

"For my part," said Miss Spuytenduyvil, with a candor that had not a hint of flirtation in its bald plainness, "I have decidedly missed you."

"Is it possible?" he returned. "I thought you had another gentleman to talk with." And at once his eye scanned an elderly man, with a yellow, sinewy face and a bristly, red moustache, who was talking to a lady on his other side, saying something that made her laugh, and laughing himself while he did so.

Miss Spuytenduyvil gave a toss of the head. In any one else it would have been a quick motion. In her it was as prolonged as the spreading of a peacocks tail.

"Oh, yes," she said, in very low tones, and with a brief, cruel sneer, "that is Mr. Binghamton. He took me in, as you saw. It was either very unkind or very forgetful in my cousin to let him do so. I dislike him exceedingly. I have never met him before this evening, but I dislike him, all the same. I have heard about him; I know who he is. He writes for newspapers; he is an Englishman, I believe, but a sort of adventurer. He is recognized; he is received; he is considered very clever, I am told; but nobody knows anything about him, except that he gets to places."

This struck Wainwright as the very high-tide mark of Miss Spuytenduyvil's uncompromising snobbery. He burst into a laugh which he felt almost reckless about having interpreted as too loud for civility; and just then, signal from their hostess, all the ladies rose to leave the room.

"You make me anxious to meet this Mr. Binghamton," said Wainwright, as he drew back Miss Spuytenduyvil's chair, and stood for a moment beside her.

She gave one of her neat, metallic smiles. "I dare say I have shocked you by some of my ideas," she replied, smoothing the folds of her dress with one narrow, frail hand.

"Oh, no," said Wainwright, laughing again; "I like ideas."

She looked at him closely for an instant, with her steady, rayless eyes. "Very few people like mine. I'm not popular. I don't want to be. I say what I think; I show my dislikes, and I have a good many dislikes. But that isn't so much my fault as society's. I am a person with a quarrel against society. I think affairs are being shamefully mismanaged there, and I insist that I have a greater right than most people to be sorry about it."

The ladies were already gliding from the room. Miss Spuytenduyvil moved away, after this speech, and Wainwright saw, as she was disappearing, that her figure had so bony an angularity as to make the fashionable robe which she wore sag and wrinkle in a sort of splendid despair that it should fit her so ill.

As the gentlemen again took their seats, Wainwright looked about him. The table had lost its chief source of genial brilliancy with the departure of the ladies. A darkness had just settled upon the feast; it was the darkness of modishly-tailored broadcloth. There had followed that ceremonious silence, too, which is so apt to result, on occasions like this, from the withdrawal of feminine forms and voices.

Wainwright sat for a few moments, without addressing a word to any one. Indeed, he had the traditional reserve of the country in which he had dwelt so long; he was surrounded by strangers. At the same time, he had no feeling of awkwardness. New and engrossing thoughts occupied him. He was thinking of Miss Spuytenduyvil; he was doing more; he was ruminating upon the extraordinary and unknown conditions that must have produced her and others with whom he saw her associated. Was this the America which had familiarized itself to his indifferent ken, while overseas, by a sort of robust banner-waving and a noisy declaration of liberty and equality for all? Were these dainty figures, which might have bowed in a Queen's Drawing Room of lounged at a London club, actually Americans?

Wainwright was still looking about him. The gentlemen were beginning to talk to each other, with a quiet and careless ease. A servant had supplied him with a cigar, and set a waxen taper in tempting proximity to it. Other cigars were being lighted from other waxen tapers, at right and left. It was now that Wainwright for the first time experienced, by reason of his isolation, a slight sense of embarrassment. But a touch fell upon his shoulder immediately afterward. He looked round, and saw Mr. Bodenstein.

"I want to present you to Mr. Binghamton," said his host.

In another moment, Wainwright found himself shaking hands with the red-moustached, yellow-visaged gentleman whom Miss Spuytenduyvil had just condemned so roundly.

III.

MR. BINGHAMTON at once began to talk. He had a little reddish-hazel eye, which rarely met yours for more than a second at a time. He spoke with a very English intonation, and with galloping rapidity. Sometimes he would give his moustache a sudden vigorous pull, as though he were correcting it for some misdemeanor. He was Smoking a cigarette, and blowing forth most of the smoke through the nostrils of his small, solid nose, whose end took an impudent upward curve.

"I'm tremendously glad to meet you, Mr. Wainwright," he said. "Hear you've been living on the other side for an age. In the old country, too, as we Englishmen say. You don't intend to stop here long, I'm told. But perhaps you'll get used to it here, and like it. Let me present Mr. Carroll Gansevoort."

Wainwright now shook hands with a young gentleman of slender, shapely figure, dark, expressive eyes, and hair brushed with glossy neatness from either side of an exceedingly exact parting. Wainwright had seen a good many young Englishmen who looked, when in evening dress, very much like Mr. Gansevoort. The latter wore a large gold fob pendant from a black ribbon under his low-cut waistcoat, and the white width of his shirt-bosom revealed but a single stud, made of one fine pearl. He had shoes that came almost to a sharp point at either end, and shone with the effective radiance of superfine patent leather. On one delicate hand was a seal ring, into which a crest and arms had been graven; on the small finger of the other hand was a heavy gold band, in which sparkled a large sunken diamond. Mr. Gansevoort had an extremely lounging manner; the muscles of his tall, slight frame appeared in a perpetual state of laxity. He sat with legs crossed one moment, and with an arm thrown over the back of his chair the next. He was smoking a cigar, which he transferred from hand to hand in graceful unrest. He was always graceful, just as he was always restless. But it promptly occurred to Wainwright that his manner was imitative, factitious, as though he had modeled it after some admired British type. When he spoke, which he at once did, the English pronunciation was so perfectly rendered in his speech that Wainwright, with his experienced ear, could scarcely tell why he should not feel certain that Mr. Gansevoort was an Englishman. But he somehow felt most doubtful on that point, without clearly being able to explain his doubt.

"I heard Binghamton say that you had just come over," began this young gentleman, with a civility that had the air of being rather seldom given. "You must have got awfully used to it there by this time."

"Oh, yes," said Wainwright, "I am very used to it."

"England's such an enormously jolly place." continued Mr. Gansevoort. "This country is a beastly hole in comparison. I've no doubt you think so already, don't you, now?"

Wainwright started as this last question was put to him. "No, I do not, really," he said with decision.

Mr. Binghamton broke into a laugh. "Good!" He exclaimed. "It isn't a beastly hole a bit. Gansevoort, here, is always running it down."

Mr. Gansevoort had, by this time, turned toward some one on his other side, and begun a new conversation. Mr. Binghamton lowered his voice and went on addressing Wainwright. "Try a glass of this Burgundy, won't you? Yes? That's right. Bodenstein's famous for his Burgundy; well, for the matter of that, no one ever got a drop of bad wine in this house. He has a *chef,* too, that can't be matched anywhere, even in Paris. You saw what the dinner was. That is the way he al ways does these things. . . . .Your health, Mr. Wainwright; may you take a liking to your mother country."

"I have never disliked her, said Wainwright, drinking some of his wine. "But I am afraid that I have been indifferent to her."

Mr. Binghamton laughed again. His tawny face broke into little wrinkles when he laughed, making him look jocose even to. grotesqueness. "Bless my soul!" he said "it's the fashion to be that, nowadays."

"I did not know it was the fashion," replied Wainwright, more seriously than he knew. "At least," he added, "not here."

"Oh, yes, indeed. But it's all terrible nonsense, you know. Have you never heard of such a thing as an Anglo-maniac?

"Never."

"Well, you'll see a few specimens quite soon. Our friend Gansevoort is one. I think Gansevoort would consider himself disgraced if he wore a pair of trousers or carried an umbrella that was not of English make."

"Truly you astonish me! And are there many people in this country who resemble him?"

Mr. Binghamton seemed inclined to laugh again. But, instead, he blew a great deal of cigarette smoke through his odd little nose. "There is a large clique of men whose members resemble him. For instance, most of his associates are cut out of the same cloth. But I see a lot of people who take very different views. I go into half a dozen sets, you know. I'm a man about town. By Jove, I think I know more of what New York is than one New Yorker out of five hundred, Englishman born though I am. I'm acquainted with every body, you see; I make a point of it; I enjoy it."

Wainwright gave a sly smile. "From what I heard not long ago," he said, "I was led to infer that one could not be on good terms with our host and hostess if he were acquainted with everybody.

Mr. Binghamton looked puzzled for a moment; then, employing one of his quick, jerky gestures, he seized Wainwright's arm, leaning forward with a humorous

frown on his low, round forehead. "I understand" he said, in bustling semitone,—
"I understand perfectly. You mean something that dreadful Miss Spuytenduyvil
has been saying to you." Here the speaker made a wry face, that might have done
famously for a bronze statuette of Comedy, so ludicrous was its funny distortion.
"By Jove my dear fellow, that girl is my simple abomination. The idea of my having
to take her in to dinner! It was positively ghastly. Now, I assure you, I'm not apt to
speak ill of people; I'm immensely **commode;** I make he best of everybody I meet,
and I manage to get a great deal of real enjoyment out of my dealings with all society. But that girl gives me a feeling, when I'm near her, of sitting in a draught and
wantonly catching cold. I've avoided her for months; to-night, as you see, our introduction to each other became fatality. I would as soon have carried a death's head
in to dinner. I positively think she has been constructed on a framework of bones
taken from her own family vault. I don't believe she has got any pulse. I shouldn't
be surprised if there were a little hole in the back of her head, where she put a key
every morning, and wound up the clockwork that serves her for an intelligence.
She despises me because she has no knowledge of my grand father; she values everybody according to his grandfather. . . . Good heavens! what a service hers would
have done his kind, if he had only remained a bachelor!

Mr. Binghamton had removed his hand from Wainwright's arm some little
time ago, but the latter now placed his own hand, in a softly jovial way, upon the
Englishman's shoulder. There was something about this Mr. Binghamton that did
more than merely amuse him Wainwright perceived a heartiness in the mar which
seemed to spring from something appreciably actual. He had already told himself,
with his alert sense at noting and valuing character, that the sincerity might not be
deep or strong. Here was a sort of professional diner-out, a person of the most light,
worldly pattern. But so far as he went, though the distance might not be far, Mr.
Binghamton was at least real, spontaneous and genuine.

"Upon my word," Wainwright now said, "I don't want to have Miss Spuytenduyvil described to me. I have already drawn my own rather painful impressions
of her. I should much prefer knowing, if you've no objections, whether, of the half
a dozen sets which you frequent, these guests of to-night represent the most select
set; and if so, why."

Mr. Binghamton laughed again. "You look prodigiously in earnest," he said.

"You seem like a man thirsting for information."

"You are quite right there."

Mr. Binghamton drooped his head in apparent reflection, though the corner of his mouth twitched somewhat mirthfully. On a sudden be raised his head again. Each little hazel eye beamed forth from a kind of merry squint.

"It's amusing," he said, "to find any one who dines with the Bodensteins, and yet who wants to be told why they are such horrible swells."

"Miss Spuytenduyvil said something of the same sort, was Wainwright's quiet reply.

"Oh, bother Miss Spuytenduyvil!" returned Mr. Binghamton, leaning over to empty his glass. "The mere mention of her name chills my Burgundy. . . . How shall I gratify your perfectly natural curiosity?" he went on, giving Wainwright one of his transient sidelong looks. "Well, when our host first came here he was the plainest of nobodies. I believe he is a Hungarian; in one way he was certainly a Bohemian, if you'll pardon my bad joke. He had drifted into a well-known banking-house,—Heaven knows how! There he started as a banker for himself, under the patronage of a celebrated German capitalist,—Heaven knows how, again! All this while he had been struggling to make the influential people receive rum. They tell queer stories of how he was rebuffed. But he persevered. He had made up his mind to be a grandee. He is a person who needs only to make up his mind that he will do a thing to succeed in it. He sets his teeth, gives a leap, and clears the hurdle, however high it is. The finest *coup* that he ever made was his marriage. All that he required was to marry brilliantly. He had got himself received everywhere, he had become a person of consequence, it is true, but his foot-hold still wanted firmness. And at last he married Miss Amsterdam. She had been the belle of the past season; she had twenty thousand a year in her own right; she had refused ten other men in as many months, to my certain knowledge. But Bodenstein won her, all the same. They say that he settled a million upon her to do it. Even then, some of her family made a fuss about the marriage."

"Miss Spuytenduyvil, for instance," said Wainwright, with a smile.

"Bah! that caricature doesn't count. She's of no importance at all; She's merely a poor relation of a great family, who tries to increase her value in the world by making herself the most obnoxious of snobs."

"It seems rather strange," said Wainwright, to hear of a great American family."

"But they exist, I assure you. Not politically great, as in Europe, of course. The Amsterdams have no seat in any House of Peers but they are a very proud and powerful race, notwithstanding. They go straight back through the Revolution to the times when New York was a Dutch village. And every day this influence of family becomes a stronger force here. New people with big fortunes and no descent look with envious eyes at certain doors that remain coldly closed against them. This may seem like a frightfully incongruous thing in the largest city of the largest republic on the globe; but there isn't the slightest doubt about it as a fact. The American social scheme, in nearly all its chief cities, at least, is often a most amusing satire upon itself. All the people whom you've met tonight think quite as much of their 'positions' (Judged relatively, of course) as the haughtiest *vieille noblesse* in Europe."

Very soon afterward, the gentlemen abandoned their smoking and went to join the ladies in the drawing-rooms. Mr. Carroll Gansevoort walked at Wainwright's side.

"I saw Binghamton firing away at you," he said, in his loitering voice, "and knew that no fellow had a chance to talk while he was doing that sort of thing. But he's confoundedly clever, is Binghamton. Upon my word, now, he knows a fearful lot. By the way, did you bring any traps over with you? I suppose not, eh? I've just had a jolly drag sent across. It's going to beat anything in the Coaching-Club, I fancy. We've a Coaching-Club here, you know. Nothing so swell as yours, of course. . . . I say, can't I present you to any more of these ladies? That little girl with the red hair, now, . . . she's ever so pretty when one gets nearer to her. She's a great catch, and awfully good form; you see how the men are flocking up to her. They say she owns a whole street somewhere, I think it's Philadelphia. One doesn't know much about her people; she was taken up a good deal last summer at Newport. Pray let me present you; she's horribly fond of Englishmen."

But Wainwright expressed his intention of departing after he should say a few words to Mrs. Bodenstein. Then he lightly touched Mr. Gansevoort's arm, and added.

"By the way, I must beg you to remember that I am not an Englishman. I am an American." After that, he paused for a second or two, and looked full into the serene, patrician face of his companion. "Yes," he went on, "I am an American, like yourself."

He had, somehow, not been able to resist that mildly reproachful sarcasm. He left soon afterward, went back to his hotel, and sat for some time, consuming another cigar and thinking. He felt that he had much to think about. On the whole, his meditations were more satisfactory than a longer sojourn would have been among the grandeurs of the Bodenstein mansion. He was not sorry that he had avoided knowing the young lady with red hair, who owned a whole street somewhere, and had so marked a preference for Englishmen. He was under the impression that he had met enough people for one day, and had had enough surprises. And while he sat ruminating upon his recent experiences and the keenness of their suggestions, he felt like one who has abruptly confronted a problem of baffling novelty.

IV.

A GREATER portion of the next day Wainwright spent with his lawyers. In the evening he resolved to go and see Mrs. Townsend Spring. New York had begun by amazing him; it had ended by sharply interesting him. He was not yet sure whether he liked it or not. He had still seen but a corner of the picture; more drapery, so to speak, must be withdrawn, for the *ensemble* to come clearly forth. And he found himself quite eager to observe the picture from the most advantageous of stand-points and with eyes of critical impartiality. He had never chosen to mingle greatly in English fashionable circles. Had he done so, he would doubtless have met there a few Americans of both sexes whose refinement and good breeding would have prepared him, however insufficiently, for the facts which had of late burst upon his knowledge. As it was, he had lived, in England, a life midway between that of the pomp-loving aristocrat and the scholarly recluse. He had his lodgings in London, well appointed, not exempt from some of the best DOOKS, journals, and magazines; he had enjoyed his club and his club associates; he had stayed at country houses; he had shot in the season; he had dined out considerably when in town, and not been above an occasional crowded ball while the dowagers and the marketable beauties were down from the country in full feather. Briefly, he had seen all that is most English in English life, and hence had naturally breathed into his being that insularity of thought and feeling which accompanies any such mode of passing one's days. During his trip through Switzerland he had met Mrs. Spring, and had liked her as we so often like what presents to us a new vista of observation. She had seemed to him excessively new. Her buoyant piquancy, as he then called it, had corresponded with the freshness of the scenes in which he found her. He was now anxious to see how she would strike him amid her native surroundings. He already had a suspicion that he would regard her with more exacting eyes than formerly. She had then appeared to him as an agreeable curiosity; he had perhaps unconsciously made allowances for her. She then merely served for an entertaining companion of travel, whom he had regarded with the gracious and extenuating self-admission that she was, after all, only an American lady. How would she affect him now? What sort of detail would she make in the large view that was gradually unfolding to him its panoramic entirety? As they climbed mountains together, her laugh had rung out through the limpid Alpine air with a silvery concordance. Her daring speeches, her abrupt impertinences, had harmonized with the rugged sheerness of neighboring cliffs. She had been delightfully un-English then, and so was Switzerland. But looked at with analyzing coolness against an altered background, Wainwright had strong misgivings lest she would appear quite a different figure.

A little before eight o clock, this evening, he left his hotel, which was situated in what we call the lower portion of Fifth Avenue, amid that region of residences which lack, the gallant thrift of others lying beyond them, yet wear a time-touched gravity rare in a city so roughly subversive of all memorial charm. He observed this trait of variation as he walked along; he had already marked it under the less dubious conditions of daylight. The January weather had recently changed, with that instability which, till of late, has defied even the prophecy of our scientists. All sting had left the atmosphere; a faint south wind was blowing, laden with a peculiar clamp blandness; the stars beamed above the town in a sort of rounded calm, shorn of all icy glitter. As Wainwright moved onward, the extreme peace of his environment forcibly struck him. Here was no strident roll of the omnibus; on either side the sweep of lamplit street gleamed nearly bare of passers; the houses seemed to drowse in a lazy duskiness, with infrequent squares of light at their windows. But a few hundred steps brought our observer into quite another realm. The dwellings all wore a more modern air. Before some of them stood coaches and coupés in somber torpor, doubtless waiting for occupants who were destined to distress the more punctual attendants at theatre or opera. A brief interval brought him within that spacious quarter which fronts the Fifth Avenue Hotel. Here reigned a most bustling activity. The great marble mass of the hotel lifted itself in solemn pallor against the tranquil darkness. But below, on its white, columned portico, was a throng of men, smoking and talking together. Wainwright paused for a moment, and looked about him. Madison Square lay upon his left, showing the black. traceries of its leafless trees. In a broad interspace, filled with the busy jingle of gliding street-cars and the active rumble of carriages, rose an immense lamp, whose cluster of illumined globes shed cordial radiations upon the shadowy movements beneath. Directly in front of where Wainwright had stationed himself, and across the intervening street, juts a wedge of building that is the point of intersection between this noted avenue and the still more popular domain of Broadway. The structure is low, and overtopped by the wall of one closely behind it. On a square of can vas reared above its roof, a gigantic disc of light had been thrown, evidently by means of some concealed magic-lantern. An extraordinary entertainment was now taking place, for the benefit of any one who chose to regard it. At one moment huge letters appeared to start forth from vacuum upon the disc, telling the beholder with a sort of mercantile ghostliness where he could procure the most durable shirts. Then this elfin communication would vanish, to be replaced by a colossal old man asleep in a chair, with jaws moving weirdly, and a mouse crawling at stealthy pace toward the movable aperture. At last the mouse entered it, and was vigorously chewed up, to the delight of gigging by-standers. Instantly afterward this dramatic event became blank nothingness, and was succeeded by the miraculous-looking information that Tompkins the tailor never disappointed a customer. Wainwright watched it all with soft amazement. He presently passed onward, with a sense of having encountered a new local incident. Perhaps he failed to appreciate how intensely characteristic of his native country was the sight he had just witnessed. He had not vet discovered that the advertising impulse, in our special form of civilization, may sometimes reach hysterical points of assertiveness.

Leaving the little fascinated throng, Wainwright continued his walk. He passed the big crowded porch. All sorts of men seemed thronging there. A rough, grisly person in a draggled ulster stood next one with a dyed moustache waxed at either end, a hard, animal face, a heavy rope of watch-chain, and an enormous diamond flashing from his shirt-front. Quiet figures, pompous figures, and threadbare figures were all heterogeneously grouped here. He cast a momentary look into the wide hall beyond, and saw that it was peopled with a dense, restless multitude. He had a sense of being engirt almost to a degree of violence by the chafe and fret of life. At the same instant a thought crossed him of how he had lived for years quite heedless that the social elements had even existed which wrought so much robust tumult. These had been shaping out their destiny, so to speak, and he had thought nothing about them. A. realization of his own indifferent absence abruptly stung him like a twinge of conscience. He could scarcely explain the feeling; it was too elusive and unsolicited. He had a sort of odd premonition that he might perhaps explain it better hereafter. For the present, it seemed to bear grim yet vague kinship to self-accusation, if not positive remorse.

He laughed low to himself as he walked on, and in truth the laugh might have rung a little harsh if it had been more audible.

"I don't know what I am coming to," he told his own thoughts. "Shall I suspect myself of being ashamed that I am on such distant terms with my own country?"

He had slight difficulty in finding Mr. Spring's residence. It was a basement house, with one large lighted window, whose drawn shade bore the reflected like-ness, outlined in delicate photography, of tropical foliage growing from a slender-pedestaled urn. He gave this window a brief yet contemplative glance before ringing the bell. Its brilliancy and breadth had something that reminded him of Mrs. Spring herself. But there the analogy stopped. That bit of aerial picturesque ness limned upon the radiant surface by no means suggested his prospective hostess. It seemed to imply a covert and subtle grace of which he did not recall that her best mood had ever been capable. If the flat, bold splendor of the window-pane represented Mrs. Spring, he had a quaint fancy that the slim bouquet of dreamy leafage might speak with tender prophecy for some unseen inmate of her household.

A maid-servant admitted him, clad in an ample white apron and a. fluted cap that was French without being coquettish. The maid took his card, and parted the expanse of a rich amber curtain, while he was doffing his outward attire. He had time to perceive that the narrow hall possessed several other exits, and that each was draped with stately uniformity in the same delicious amber material, while the carpet beneath his feet had the hue, depth and softness of moss. Almost immediately he heard voices behind the nearest fall of tapestry, and when the servant presently ushered him between its folds he discovered that the chamber lying beyond contained a group of people. It was not a large apartment, and its occupants, of whom three were ladies and three gentlemen, gave it a deceptive air of being overcrowded. It reminded the new-comer of pictures that he had seen by Toulmouche or De Jonghe. He had a confused impression of Oriental screens, deep-cushioned chairs, vivid-colored rugs, and tables and shelves literally piled with bric-a-brac. The three gentlemen all rose as he entered, and one of the ladies tried to rise, but fell back into her capacious arm-chair with a little shriek of laughter, as her foot struck against an elaborate golden-bronze coal-scuttle near the merrily-crackling fire.

This lady, as Wainwright now saw, was none other than Mrs. Townsend Spring herself. She held out to him a small, plump hand, as white as milk, while leaning back in her chair with mirthful abandonment. She had a round face of infantile freshness, whose red lips seemed made as though meant always to curl in laughter over teeth of dazzling purity. Her little figure was modeled with an exuberance imperiling symmetry, if not j spoiling, it.

Wainwright took the hand she offered him; she retained it for several moments, shaking it while she laughed and spoke at the same time. He was obliged to stoop rather awkwardly during this prolonged process of welcome, for his hostess wore a silken robe of much splendor, whose copious train had got itself coiled before her chair, leaving visible two tiny feet in high-heeled suppers.

"It was ever so nice of you to come so soon!" cried Mrs. Spring, letting her jocund face beam up at her guest from a tufted background of black and scarlet embroidery. "I was never more amazed than when Townsend told me you had come to this country." Here Mrs. Spring looked at one of the three gentlemen, who still remained standing. "Do put that coal-scuttle where it belongs!" she exclaimed, and while a great burst of laughter left her lips she gave the article referred to a vigorous kick with one of her dainty feet. "I think you placed it there purposely to trip me up," she went on, with a sudden mock gravity in face and tone, "just because I ordered you to feed the fire. I don't see how anybody who is always playing polo and riding races, and all that, can be so revengefully lazy. You don't deserve to have me introduce you to the best fellow in the world. Upon my word, it would be a good way of punishing you.

Mrs. Spring still retained Wainwright's hand. She now gave it a final exaggerated shake, that would have looked an act of shocking boldness if her diminutive stature and peculiar, insolent sort of felicity had not combined to make nearly everything of the sort that she did irresistibly comic.

"I hope you don't mean that I am the best fellow in the world," said Wainwright, at this point, with a laugh that hid his pardonable embarrassment. "I should be very sorry to come among strangers with the necessity of living up to any such monstrous reputation."

A general laugh followed these words, and then a voice at Wainwright's elbow immediately said, in brisk tones which he recognized, even before turning and meeting the speaker's face, "I trust you don't mean to count me as a stranger."

"Oh, far from that," said Wainwright, genially, as he found himself shaking hands with Mr. Binghamton.

"Upon my word," declared Mrs. Spring, in her rattling, crisp way, as she looked at Wainwright and waved one hand toward Mr. Binghamton, "I didn't suppose for an instant that you could have been twenty-four hours in New York without knowing that man. Nobody ever escapes him for a longer period. He goes to eight and ten different places of a night There's a sort of ghost-story told about him that he was once in two separate drawing-rooms at precisely the same hour. They say that he waits at the wharves for the foreign steamers to come in, and gets the custom-house officers to introduce him to newly-landed celebrities."

Mr. Binghamton heard this tirade with a look of such complete unconcern as no facial adroitness could have counterfeited. "You see what an important being Mrs. Spring evidently considers me," he said to Wainwright, "when she will postpone your introduction to no less than four of the people present simply because she has a caprice for making sport of me. But I shall repair her incivility," he continued, taking a few steps in the direction of two ladies who were seated at either end of an immense cashmere-covered lounge. "Let me present Mr. Wainwright to Miss Ruth Cheever, a sister of our hostess, and also to Miss Lydia Spring, a sister of her absent husband, whom I believe you know."

Mrs. Spring here gave one of her loud, musical laughs. "Dear me, Bing," she cried, show delightfully explanatory you are! You'd better tell the age of each young lady, while you are dealing with other personal particulars."

Mr. Binghamton closed his eyes and placed one hand upon his breadth of spotless shirt-bosom. His dry yellow face became ridiculously solemn; his jaunty red moustache seemed to acquire an absurd droop. "There are some mysteries," he said, with a voice like a slow bass chant, "which the most daring curiosity must be content to leave unsolved."

The young lady called Miss Lydia Spring here slightly tossed her head. It was a very pretty head; its curly blond hair and the waxen, pink-cheeked face beneath it had the sort of doll-like charm that we sometimes see in a coiffeurs window. She had a large, heavy, indolent figure, whose generous curves were not lessened by a raiment of some diaphanous texture, so cut as to leave in almost audacious relief the soft, creamy outlines of neck and bosom. She spoke in a petulantly arch way, while remoulding to suit her lazy mood a great plush cushion, as crimson as a garnet, upon which one of her fair, tapering arms had rested with handsome effect.

"My age isn't any mystery, if you please, she exclaimed. "I was eighteen my last birthday, and you know it perfectly well, Bing, you horrid, tormenting fellow! "Here Miss Lydia fixed a pair of babyish blue eyes on Wainwright's face. "Mr. Wainwright," she went on, "you can see now why my sister-in-law pitches into him so. One has to pitch into him to keep him from abusing one."

"And pray why is Miss Ruth, there, not indignant that I should have called her age a mystery?" asked Mr. Binghamton, at this point, with a gesture toward the young lady at the other end of the lounge.

"Oh, you had best not bring my good-nature into discussion, now said Miss Ruth Cheever, with quiet protest. "That is something which nobody should depend upon too rashly."

Wainwright turned and looked at this speaker the moment that her voice sounded. His eyes scanned her longer than he possibly knew. He liked her voice; it was full of a silvery refinement. She seemed quite of a different world from either of her relatives: the elder, with her saucy, graceful buoyancy, and the younger, with her childish mannerisms and slangy idioms.

"Lyddy is getting very ill-natured, I'm afraid, said Mr. Binghamton, with a grimace, warming himself before the fire, while Wainwright dropped into a chair midway between Mrs. Spring and her two kinswomen. "The heartless world is spoiling her; the butterfly-dust has been taken off her wines."

"You mustn't call me Lyddy," asserted Miss Spring, with a combined pout and shrug. "Must he, Fanny?" she proceeded, appealing to the wife of her brother. "It makes me seem bad style. I don't like it a bit."

"No, Bing, you mustn't," said Mrs. Spring, using a brusque seriousness that oddly contrasted with her recent jollity. She spoke the words with a sidelong look in Mr. Binghamton's direction; immediately afterward she turned the keen, small eyes, which were too small and keen to be the best feature of her blithe face, full upon Wainwright. She lowered her voice, addressing herself exclusively to him. The others seemed to take their cue, as it were, from this cool, distinct expression of preference. The gentleman who had just replaced the impeding coal-scuttle at her command, now seated himself near Miss Cheever; another gentleman had sunk into a chair, some moments ago, very close to one of Miss Spring's rosy elbows. Mr. Binghamton continued to warm himself before the fire. A hum of voices at once rose from the five people thus disposed. Meanwhile Mrs. Spring had signified to Wainwright, by an imperative little gesture, that she wished his chair drawn nearer to her own, and tie had promptly honored this tacit order.

"You don't know how glad I am that you came," she began, in her new, moderated voice. "I was literally dying to see you when I heard you had arrived. We had such a glorious time in Europe last summer, didn't we? We got along so well together, there; I hope we shall be just as good friends here. But you will seem so different here. You will be like a picture that has lost its frame."

"Oh, I shall hope soon to find another," said Wainwright, laughing, and, perhaps, a better one.

"Pshaw, my dear man, you don't know what you are saying. You will be so bored here in a week or two that you will wish it were possible to be telegraphed back again through the ocean cable. I know just how it will affect you. You will think it new and strange at first, and rather like it. Then you will finish by detesting it. They always finish by detest mg it. I don't mean the second or third rate English, you know; I mean those who have always been among the great swells. And shall I tell you why?" Here Mrs. Spring laid her hand on Wainwright's coat-sleeve. This was one of her unconventional touches, and she had a number of them, as may already have been suspected of her. "Shall I tell you why?" she repeated. "It is because our great swells all imitate yours. Now imitations are such tiresome things. Every society ought to be original to have any charm about it. Who wants to go to Turkey and find that all the hookahs and ottomans and bow-strings and bastinadoings have been exterminated? And pray of what does our 'best society' consist? Why, simply of a general bowing-down before English customs, English ideas. We're not a bit like the models we worship, but we pretend to be, all the same. Mind you, I'm not speaking of the people whom one never meets. I suppose it's a wonderful country when we look at it from a large, democratic stand-point. But I never think of looking at it so; and you'll not, either, unless you go prowling off into the prairies, or something of that sort. If you stay in New York while you are here, you'll find that our best people will run after you a good deal. You are rich, you're a gentleman of leisure, as the phrase goes, you're enormously marriageable, and you win possibly have a fine chance of observing just how one aristocracy apes and adores the other."

Wainwright was looking closely at his companion by the time that she ended this rather autocratic monologue. "Tell me," he said, while the interest that was getting so alert with him rather quickened, "do you passively submit to be classed with so despised a multitude?"

Mrs. Spring laughingly threw back her head, showing the brilliant evenness of her teeth. Passively submit!" she repeated. "Why, good heavens, my dear boy, what do I care about it? I let myself go with the current; I unit along."

Wainwright echoed her laugh; he had slightly drooped his head; he was looking at the carpet; he spoke without raising ms eyes. "I think you steer your own way," he said, "and rather adroitly. You know just where you want to go, and you go there,—sometimes dead against tides, or even rapids."

Mrs. Spring threw herself back in the big gorgeous chair. She put her head very much on one side, and stared at Wainwright between half-closed eyes. He had lifted his own eyes, now; he' recognized the attitude; it was like meeting an old associate. In Switzerland it had seemed to him informed with a delicate originality; here, amid polite and domestic surroundings, it bristled with a vicious, operatic piquancy. He had not thought to dislike it then; now he criticised it and disliked it.

"How you take one up!" she said. "That was always your way. We have a horrid American word for it,—at least it ought to be American, it is so ugly: you nag a person. But you always do it like a gentleman; you are never ill-bred about it. I think it first made me like you."

"I shall endeavor to cultivate the vice," said Wainwright, with inscrutable gallantry.

"Of course I steer my own way, continued Mrs. Spring, suddenly taking an upright posture, and giving each arm of her chair a little decisive pound on its padded abutment. "Why should I not? I like enjoyment; I have a passion for it. I never géner myself, except unintentionally, sometimes, in seeking for amusement." Her radiant face suddenly became grave, and her observer thought that its eyes took a momentary hard keenness. "But you are very right," she went on, "to say that I steer adroitly. I'm too good a pilot to run my vessel on any quicksands; and as for the rapids you spoke of, I never take them, unless I am sure—perfectly sure—that I can shoot them.

Wainwright looked at her for a moment in silence. Then his composed face broke into a broad smile. But he remained silent. He had begun to think that if he liked Mrs. Town-send Spring less in New York than he had liked her in Switzerland, she at least interested him, after a certain way, more here than she had done there.

His companion gave an abrupt, impatient shrug. It reminded him of the shaking of a kaleidoscope. The painted bits of glass were going to assume a new pattern. "If I were a vain woman," she said, "I should tell you that you were fortunate to find me at home to-night. I am usually out. This is the sea son, you know, when everybody is usually out. But we concluded to save ourselves for the great ball to-morrow night at the Grosvenors'. By 'we' I mean my sister-in-law, Lydia, and myself. I suppose that the identity of Lydia has by this time dawned upon your conscience, notwithstanding the mental confusion that must have resulted from your dropping in among such a nest of strange people. If not, let me explain that Lydia is the young lady who recently new into a rage at Binghamton's last impertinence."

Wainwright let his eyes wander toward the couch where the two young ladies were seated; but they did not rest upon Lydia.

"Is not the other young lady a resident of your household?" he asked.

"My sister Ruth? Oh, yes. But she does not care as much for society as Lyddy and myself. She only goes out now and then."

"You and she are wonderfully unlike for two sisters."

Yes, said Mrs. Spring, lowering her voice a little unamiably. "Ruth is very clever; I dare say you might like her. But she is unfortunate in one respect.

"What is that?"

"She has not any talent for enjoying life."

It struck Wainwright, while his look still furtively watched the subject of their discussion, that perhaps Miss Ruth Cheever might possess a talent for making life enjoyable to others, when disposed actively to exert it.

He would doubtless have expressed tins opinion aloud, had not two new visitors, both of whom were gentlemen, just then entered the room. Mrs. Spring rose to receive them. Her elegant costume gave forth a rich crackle as she did so, and a dainty yet distinct jingle sounded from the profuse jewelry adorning her neck and arms.

In the general uprising that followed among the gentlemen, Wainwright found himself close to Mr. Binghamton. Isn't it funny," said the latter, in a wicked mutter, "to hear that woman rattle and tinkle whenever she moves? I once met an enemy of hers who said such a good thing about it. He said that perhaps her husband made her dress so, on the same principle as that of a farmer when he ties a bell to a cow's neck, to keep it from lumping fences and getting astray."

"I should fancy there was no danger that Mrs. Spring would jump fences," murmured Wainwright, with a smile.

"No," said Mr. Binghamton, putting his arm upon Wainwright's shoulder, and leaning so close to the latter's ear that a bristle of his coarse little moustache grazed it,—"no; she only thrusts her head through the bars, now and then, if they re a safe distance apart." He gave a low chuckle after he had said this, and faint as the sound was, his hearer caught in it a ring of spite that possibly meant vengeance for Mrs. Spring's recent impudent attack. Immediately afterward, he changed his tone, however, and went on in a galloping whisper: "She's a nice enough little woman, in her way, and I don't wish her a bit of harm. Now and then she says vile things to me, but she knows that I know she doesn't mean them. She hardly ever gets up anything jolly without having me; she wouldn't quarrel with me for a finger! I've done her more than one good turn, and she counts on me to do her others. Our little talk last night convinced me that you're a social observer you're looking about. Here is a family ground that will repay lots of study. Townsend is a horrid cad, but a complete type; you couldn't get anything more perfect of its kind. He's playing cards at the club, now; he's nearly always playing cards at the club, except when gambling in Wall Street. Lyddy is a goose; She's on the verge of a great scandal, and she hasn't brains enough to discover it. You see that man with a dark complexion and a stoop? His name is Abernethy; he's here morning, noon, and night, always dangling after Lyddy. He's a married man, with the sweetest little wife in the world, who adores him. Of course there's no real harm in Lyddy, but there's a lot of harm in him. His morals are as dark as his complexion. Fanny Spring will send him off some day, but then it will be too late, and that poor fool of a Lyddy will be roundly compromised. Now just glance at Ruth Cheever. I suppose you must have noticed her before. Isn't it absurd that she should be Mrs. Spring's own sister? She's one girl in ten thousand. There's a vacant chair near her; take it, and have a talk with her. She isn't appreciated by half the praters whom she's forced to meet, and oh, bless my soul, how magnificently she despises most of them! You may not see this at first, but I assure you it's true. She doesn't express her contempt; it escapes her unconsciously. She's one of my beliefs, that girl, though I'm not one of hers, and don't deserve to be. I'll lay you a guinea She's infernally unhappy. By Jove, She's good reason to be. You'll see why, if you see more of this remarkable family. . . . I must be off; it's past my time already. I'm promised at three more places to-night solemnly promised. I'm such a confounded gadabout, you know. Take my advice concerning Ruth Cheever, old fellow. Sit down and have a chat with her; you'll not regret it."

A moment later Mr. Binghamton was making his adieus to everybody. He first shook hands briefly with Miss Cheever, in his restive way, and then said good-night to all the others. During this process a light clamor arose, of which he seemed the mirthful object. While careless railleries were being leveled at him, he bowed himself from the room, with little abrupt pauses, fitful flashes of repartee, shrugs of the shoulder, and one or two pulls at his moustache. Meanwhile, the seat beside Miss Cheever remained vacant. This young lady was the only other occupant of the room who had not risen to join in the mock wrangle with Mr. Binghamton. Wainwright advanced, and sank into the empty chair.

"I have just been hearing some very kind things said of you, Miss Cheever, he began.

"Have you come to try and corroborate their truth r she asked, smiling.

"Oh, no," he said, I am quite willing to take them for granted. I come in a most credulous frame of mind. I am full of faith.

"Which means that you will not bear disappointment with resignation. I am sorry for that."

Wainwright drew his chair a little nearer to Miss Cheever.

"I am sure that I shall not be disappointed," he said, and that if anyone is to cultivate resignation it should be yourself."

V.

MR. SPRING had by this time resumed her arm-chair, Miss Lydia, having left the lounge, had betaken herself to another chair, which bore a sort of decorative cousinship to that which her sister-in-law occupied. Three of the gentlemen had gathered about Mrs. Spring, and her sister-in-law was in close conversation with the fourth, this latter being the dark-complexioned personage who had recently roused Mr. Binghamton's caustic comments.

Wainwright's new companion slowly answered his last words. "You forget that I am prepared for you," she said. "I have heard of you beforehand. When my brother in-law mentioned, yesterday, that you had crossed the ocean, his wife burst into quite a little rhapsody about you.

"Ah," said Wainwright, "that makes us quits, does it not? We form each other's acquaintance under the most cheerful auspices. We should slip right into each other's good graces, bringing such fine credentials, being both so highly recommended, as it were."

Miss Cheever laughed. "You take it for granted," she said, "that I have implicit trust in my sister Fanny's endorsements."

Wainwright felt that he plainly detected a satirical challenge in the soft, quick side-glance that accompanied these words. His companion had already prepossessed him, as we know. She was tall, with a slight figure, of rounded flexibility. Her hair had in it the auburn shine of a frosted oak-leaf, and flowed back in thick, pliant waves from a broad white forehead. Her eyes looked black in the present light, but a near view of them made a blue sparkle steal from their shadows. Her face was of tender coloring and sensitive outline, but its features bore no especial nicety of mould or finish; they had something that was firm enough to be strength and thoughtful enough to seem intellectuality, yet their vigor was like the delicacy of those more rugged ferns that join a sweet hardihood with the slenderness of more fragile kindred.

It was now Wainwright's turn to laugh. "Oh," he said, "if you distrust a certificate of good behavior when signed by your sister, why should not I have an equal right to cast doubt upon Mr. Binghamton's credibility?"

"You have every right in the world," she, answered; and the smile that went with this response puzzled him by its rich, fleet brightness.

"Can you mean that you are not anxious to be spoken well of by Mrs. Spring?" he asked.

She looked at him steadily and rather seriously. Wainwright had a severe misgiving lest he had spoken with inadmissible boldness. But the recollection of Mr. Binghamton's words was still very fresh in his mind, and even these few brief moments of Miss Cheever's society had sharpened his sense of how great a contrast lay between herself and the light, unconventional woman who was her near relation.

"I would rather my sister should speak well than ill of me," answered the young girl.

"That is a very ambiguous reply. Do you Know, pursued Wainwright, that when I heard you were Mrs. Spring's sister I could at first scarcely believe it?"

Miss Cheever slowly nodded her head. "The relationship surprises a good many people, she returned.

"And is my surprise to increase or diminish, after I have known you better?"

She started, like a person quite thrown off guard. She spoke at once, with a gentle impetuosity. "I am sure that you will find no point of resemblance between us," she said, and then paused, flushing a little.

"Ah," said Wainwright, "that is pleasant to hear. We always like to have our first impressions of people confirmed by experience, you know."

She looked interested, and the look became her charmingly. "Pray tell me just what was your first impression of me. I am curious to learn it."

Wainwright shook his head; he appeared humorously distressed. "It might annoy you," he said.

"That only makes my curiosity the stronger," she replied, leaning a little nearer to him. 'If you annoy me I shan't hold you at fault. I shall have brought the catastrophe upon myself, and shall have been the victim of my own curiosity."

Wainwright seemed to reflect. "Well," he presently announced, "I concluded that you were a young lady dissatisfied with her surroundings."

"You were perfectly right," said Miss Cheever, with calm emphasis. She bent her auburn head for a moment, and rearranged a knot of flowers at her bosom. Then she looked up at Wainwright with great steadiness "I have not lived here very long, she went on. "It is only two years since I came. I used to live with my mother, in a simple Massachusetts town. It was not far from Boston,—just near enough to be civilized." And then a touch of laughter broke her modulated voice.

"Ah," said Wainwright, handsomely, "it must have been a suburb."

"It was very pleasant. A little provincial, perhaps, but it had what you call a 'tone;' it was delightfully respectable. I left some dear friends there. When mother died I was forced to come and live with Fanny, who had already been married several years to Mr. Spring. The change was decisive. I don't think I have ever got used to it. I don't think I ever shall get used to it." . . . Her eyes, still meeting her companion s, had the same contemplative fixity, but a wistful spark had somehow stolen into the liquid gloom of each. "I often grow vexed and out of patience with myself at my own dire failure."

"I really can't see why!" exclaimed Wainwright, with more warmth than he was perhaps aware of.

Miss Cheever clasped her hands together with a pretty gesture of impatience, and let them rest thus in her lap. "Oh, the air is so full of sarcasms, now, about the young woman who wearies for a wider sphere, and all that. There is so much more worldly wisdom in making the best of things. A woman gets no satisfaction, in this age, out of the most legitimate discontentments. She has a choice between two extremes, and that is all. She must either consign herself to frivolities, or else be satirized as a prig, a person 'with views'. And in either case she is satirized, I find, all the same. Those cruelly clever people who write the Saturday reviews will not let her escape from the domain of ridicule. Now I hate to be laughed at, even by people whom I despise. I could stand their frowns or their sneers much better. I can give you no idea of what chagrin it causes me to know that many of my sister's friends criticise me as 'rather superior.' To be rather superior, with them, is much the same as if one should have a bonnet that was in bad taste. I have the most feminine disgust for a bonnet in bad taste. And so I take the first extreme, in a sort of desperation. I exert myself to be as frivolous as I can. I am morbidly afraid of being relegated among the spectacled reformers. The attitude of championizing my own sex doesn't at all suit me. I am not sure that the sex needs to be championized; I am in hopes that it will secure all it deserves in a less melodramatic way. So you see that my position—though I don't know if you care to see anything about my position—is a kind of cowardly compromise."

"I care a great deal," said Wainwright with direct candor. "But I confess," he went on, "that I must hear your case defended a little before I quite understand its peculiar grievances. I have no doubt that you can make an able defense. I am already enlisted among your sympathizers, so to speak. You shall probably find me a most willing convert."

Miss Cheever raised her brows as he ended, and he thought that a soft flash left her eyes; he was sure indeed that the mobile line of her mouth took an almost stern curve. Her voice, when she spoke, had a piqued ring that wholly confirmed his first swift impression of having unwittingly wounded her.

"Really," she exclaimed, "you treat me as if I were openly posing for a martyr! Pray be assured that I meant to do nothing of the sort."

"I didn't suspect you of it," said Wainwright, with fluent apology. "Please pardon me if in siding with your opinions my zeal was too premature to be discreet."

Before she could answer this diplomatic stroke of courtesy, Mrs. Spring was heard calling across the room. "I am not going to let Ruth monopolize you!" cried the little lady to Wainwright. "Let me make you know these gentlemen," she continued, sweeping one hand toward her three surrounders, who all rose and bowed as she dashed off their names. It struck Wainwright, as he also rose and bowed, that the three gentlemen were all strongly similar in appearance. Each was blond, each slender, and each in full evening dress. "They're all frightfully English in their tastes," continued Mrs. Spring, referring to this elegant young trio, "so you ought to like them."

The three young gentlemen laughed. They each laughed, as it were, to the same degree, and with some embarrassment. Then all rubbed their hands together a little, spread their legs slightly apart, leaned their elbows upon their knees, and with drooped heads exchanged covert glances of amusement.

Mrs. Spring soon broke the brief yet awkward silence that followed. "But they're enormously nice fellows," she said, still alluding to her guests. "I don't know what I should do without them; they are so good to me at parties." She was leaning back in her great chair; she had joined both hands and put them behind her head; her dimpled arms each formed a right angle; the posture would have been execrably out of taste with almost any other woman; she assumed it with a felicity that did not save it from being out of taste but freed it from offensive coarseness, and perhaps made it uniquely picturesque, "Now there is Ruth," proceeded Mrs. Spring, with merciless personality, throwing a full, bold look toward her sister. "She affects not to care a bit whether she receives attention or no. She goes in for the bored manner; don't you, Ruth, dear? I don't know how long she means to keep it up. My theory is that nothing succeeds so ill as the bored manner. Everybody thinks that he is the special object of your *ennui,* in that case, and flies from you like a plague. I am ever so much more sensible. When I'm bored in the most deadly way I cultivate my best smiles."

"I shall be afraid of you, after this, when you are particularly nice," said one of the gentlemen who sat near Mrs. Spring.

A laugh followed this speech, confined among the special group surrounding her to whom it was addressed. In the midst of the laugh Mrs. Spring made some merry retort, only audible to her own limited circle.

Just then Wainwright felt a light touch upon his arm. He turned, and saw that a new look, as eager as it was transient, had overspread Miss Cheever's face.

"My sister is in one of her unpleasant moods to-night," she said, very quickly, and below her breath. "I have a favor to ask of you."

"What is it?" he inquired.

"That you will not stay longer. I know it must seem very strange for me to ask you this. . . . But when we meet again—as I hope we shall—I will try to explain myself more clearly."

"If your sister is rude to you," persisted Wainwright, why do you not pay her back in her own coin? I am sure you are quite capable of it."

"Pray, hush!" murmured his companion. "She is looking at us even while the others are speaking to her." For a moment Ruth Cheever's eyes wore an expression of surpassing melancholy. "You wish to hear my case defended. You might do so if you remained; my sister could let you into the secret of why my surroundings satisfy me so ill. But I would rather make the defense myself, at some other time."

She spoke with great speed and very low. Her delicate chin had a pathetic quiver; something almost tragic in her face was struggling with an evident effort to appear indifferent and serene; the change was obvious to Wainwright only because of his extreme nearness. "I understand," he said, feeling an actual pang of pity.

"I am afraid Ruth is talking books to you! cried Mrs. Spring, just at this point, once more addressing Wainwright. "It's so dreadful of her to do it. She has no mercy on people."

Wainwright rose. He felt exceedingly angry. "Miss Cheever was not talking of books," he said, in his rich, gentle voice, "and I am inclined to think that she has more mercy than you have."

He at once turned and shook hands with Ruth. While she observed the action, Mrs. Spring protested against so early a departure. But Wainwright went up and shook hands with her before the protest had ended, merely saying some polite words which signified his firm intention of going at once. He then bowed to Miss Lydia, to her dark-visaged adherent, and to the gentlemen who sat near Mrs. Spring.

"I know that Ruth has frightened you away!" exclaimed his hostess. "Pray tell me what she did it with. Was it the rights of woman or mental philosophy?"

"Oh, Fanny!" cried Lydia from her corner, in piping, juvenile tones, you really ought to draw it milder with Ruth. If I were she I wouldn't stand it. I'd just give you back as good as I got!"

Miss Lydia ended these words with a pert toss of the head, and looked toward Mr. Abernethy, as u for supporting acquiescence. The latter broke into a silent laugh of great seeming amusement, and made some rapid reply, only loud enough for the young lady to whom he addressed it.

"Miss Cheever has been very far from frightening me away," said Wainwright. "Indeed, Mrs. Spring," he proceeded, "meeting your sister has created an additional inducement for me to repeat the present visit."

"Bravo! cried Lydia, clapping her hands "I do hope you *will* repeat it, if only to give Fanny a lesson in good manners." But before this courageous little shaft had flown home, so to speak, Wainwright had withdrawn from the room. Ruth Cheever's face had been the last that his look rested upon before crossing the threshhold. She was paler; she had lowered her eyes; he thought he saw the corners of her mouth quivering.

"That girl *is* a martyr," he told himself, as he was putting on his overcoat in the hall. And at the same moment he realized that he had conceived a strong dislike for Mrs. Spring.

Just as he was about to make his final exit by the hall door, he heard a grating sound outside, and suddenly felt the door itself pushed in his own direction. The next instant Mr. Townsend Spring became visible, latch-key in hand. He had on an overcoat of pale yellow cloth, studded with huge pearl buttons, and a high opera-hat tipped considerably sideways. His glimpse of white neck-tie, his brilliant boots, and his black trousers told that he was in evening costume. His face looked more flushed than when Wainwright had last seen it in the full sunlight on Broadway. He diffused a distinct odor of mingled tobacco and brandy. His manner somehow lacked its usual bluff jollity, but he showed decided warmth of welcome.

"Confound it, old fellow," he said, while shaking Wainwright's hand, "I'm devilish sorry I missed you. What are you going so soon for?"

"Oh, I have made quite a long visit," said Wainwright.

Townsend Spring took off his hat, rapidly compressed it into a state of flat collapse, and flung it upon a table at his side. He passed one hand over his forehead, for an instant, closing his eyes.

"I've been having an infernal time in Wall Street, to-day," he said. "I came home early to-night because I was so deucedly fagged out." He now abruptly placed a hand on Wainwright's shoulder, and as he did so the latter perceived a confusion in his manner and speech, whose origin seemed midway between some mental distress and the turbulence caused by undue stimulant. "I've put you down at the club," he proceeded, with the air of one who suddenly recollects an important point. "You'll get the invitation at your hotel; I ordered it sent there. We must dine there together. . . . I'll send you word when it'll be. . . . Just now I'm too bothered in

my head to name a day." Here he paused, and pointed toward the tapestried door-
way from which Wainwright had recently emerged. "Who's in there with Fanny?
he asked.

"Your sister and Miss Cheever," said Wainwright.

"Lyddy and Ruth. . . . Oh, yes, of course. I mean, are there any men?"

Wainwright tried to recollect the names of the male guests to whom he had
been presented. But the result of his effort was only to say,—

"There are three gentlemen whose names I don't recall; and there is a Mr. Abernethy, who is talking, I believe, to your sister."

"Jim Abernethy? Yes, of course," said Townsend Spring. And then he looked
down for a moment, and muttered under his ample moustache a few brief words
that were flavored with a sullen hostility. Wainwright naturally bethought himself
of what he had heard Mr. Binghamton say regarding the attentions of Mr. Abernethy to Townsend Spring's sister, and he might, under present circumstances, have
felt a keener embarrassment if it had not been evident to him that the man who
thus spoke employed only the random force of clouded faculties.

Townsend Spring's covert indignation lasted but a few seconds. His attention
was suddenly attracted by a tasteful lamp of stained glass that directly faced him,
pendent from the ceiling above, and flooding the draperied hall with delightful
radiance.

"Well, by Jove," he exclaimed, staring at the lamp, "so Fanny's done it, no matter what I said! Just like her. I knew she would. She's always buying new things for
the house. I've got to foot another big bill. I'm always footing big bills." Here the
speaker shook his head absently, with an air of doleful rumination.

Wainwright felt like shrugging his shoulders in hearty unconcern. But instead
of this he opened the hall door again, and quietly wished Townsend Spring good-
night. The latter once more grasped his hand and proposed that he should remain
longer. But Wainwright, with the most apposite excuse he could master, presently
secured an exit from the house. He walked with brisk steps for several blocks. He
was thinking of all he had seen.

"A girl of fine mind and wholesome impulses," ran his thoughts, "who is engirt
by three people quite her inferiors. Mrs. Spring is aggressive and impertinent; Lydia
is vulgar and capricious; Townsend Spring is fast and abominable. What an atmo-

sphere to breathe in!"

It is needless to state that he was thinking of Ruth Cheever. Some time after he had regained his hotel that evening, and, indeed, while composing himself to sleep, he was haunted by the memory of two sweetly sombre eyes, and stirred with an unwonted pity for one whom fate seemed schooling to fortitude under needless rigors.

VI.

AN invitation, granting him access to the Metropolitan Club, awaited Wainwright at his hotel. On the following morning he also received a card for the ball at Mrs. Grosvenor's that same evening, ac-companied by a polite note from Mr. Bodenstein, who had used his august social authority in securing this privilege.

During a greater portion of the day Wainwright was in converse with his lawyers, and he escaped from their dismal monopoly only at a late hour in the afternoon. He then returned to his hotel, dressed for the evening, and went forth to stroll in Fifth Avenue. He had gone but a short distance when he met Mr. Binghamton, walking at the side of a stout elderly lady of majestic carriage and hand some aquiline face. Mr. Binghamton was laughing and gesticulating; he appeared to be in the act of imparting to the lady some rare bit of pleasantry. The two men exchanged bows, and Wainwright passed onward. But perhaps three minutes later he heard his name rather excitedly pronounced from behind, and immediately afterward Mr. Binghamton joined him.

"I've just left Mrs. Spencer Vandervoort, said the Englishman, in his voluble way. "She's one of the cleverest women in New York; she and I are devoted friends. Did you observe her at all?"

"Yes," answered Wainwright. "She had a very striking appearance."

"Oh, of course. She looks like an English duchess, though I've seen English duchesses who were remarkably dowdy and dull. But it isn't only her appearance that makes one like her. Oh, by no means! She's so confoundedly bright. But she has her faults. They're immensely amusing faints. She's always asking favors of a fellow. It's extraordinary, the way that woman gets just what she wants out of society. ***She's*** a type, my dear Wainwright; she would amuse you. I know of five separate female friends of hers from whom she habitually secures some sort of distinct service at least once a month. Sometimes it is an opera-box; sometimes a carriage to pay off her visits in. She has a vast amount of visits to pay off. She simply knows everybody and goes everywhere. I'm not a circumstance to her, in that way. She was ill for several days last year, and on getting well she moaned to an intimate, 'Just think of it! I have missed eighteen invitations!' She is usually in perfect health, and so never misses anything. Her health is such a brilliantly fine affair that I often believe she must borrow it from somebody, as she does all the fresh novels. She goes to every new play that appears; somebody always takes her. I've taken her innumerable times; the first thing that I know she has contrived to make me ask her.

"I am curious to meet this extraordinary lady," said Wainwright.

Mr. Binghamton gave a short laugh as they walked on. "Of course you will meet her," he said. "You could no more escape her than if she were a fate. Oh, she has already heard all about you. You are doomed to be at one of her Saturday evenings."

"Ah," said Wainwright; then she entertains?"

"Yes. I believe it is one Saturday every month. She gives her guests a pink drink that I have never been rash enough to taste. There is an ancient tradition that cochineal, not claret, is its chief ingredient. She is perfectly shameless about poking it at people and saying: "My punch has no to-morrow. I always feel that *I* should have none if I ventured a glass of it."

"Such unblushing economies," laughed Wainwright, "ought to impair her popularity."

"Oh, she 's abominated by a lot of people. But not specially for that reason. it's because of her clever tongue, her ready wit, her really superior mind. All the fashionable fools hate her, and it's her own fault; she has no place among them. Why, that woman has the ability to organize a **salon** that might become famous. But she has never learned the art of growing old; nor has she an idea of keeping herself select. She will leave a miscellaneous gathering at Mrs. Lucretia Bateson Bangs's, the newspaper correspondent s, to attend a ball at the Bodenteins, where Amsterdams beam upon Spuytenduyvils and snobbery rules the roast."

"I suppose she will be at the Grosvenors' ball this evening, said Wainwright.

"Yes, and a lot of other places before it. She will have on a yellow dress garnished with red rosebuds. An unholy wit whom I know said that it makes her look like a blood orange. She will wear that dress right through the season at all the large entertainments. There's a notorious parsimony about it. I forgot to tell you, by the way, that her husband is a prosperous sugar-merchant."

Shortly afterward Mr. Binghamton learned that Wainwright would be among the guests at the Grosvenors' ball. "It will be a superb opportunity for you to see one of the patrician crushes," he said. He then proposed that they should dine together at the Metropolitan u, and attend the festivity later. "It's a wonder that Townsend Spring remembered to write you down at the club, he proceeded, on hearing this fact from Wainwright. "I supposed his wild Wall Street ventures must have left him awfully demoralized. It's the most extraordinary thing how he has managed to sail thus far through all financial weathers. God knows when he may strike a reef and go quite to pieces."

Wainwright turned quickly toward the speaker. "In that case," he asked, "would Miss Cheever be a sufferer?"

"Sufferer!" echoed Mr. Binghamton. He passed his arm into Wainwright's. "I don't believe the wife and sister would have a penny of their own. Townsend fell in with Fanny Cheever somewhere off in the country; I forget where it was. She was living there with her mother and Miss Ruth. The mother is dead now, and I suspect that Townsend has 'manipulated whatever slender patrimony came to the two sisters. It would go with the wreck, when the wreck occurred; there isn't a doubt of that. Mind you, I don't mean a word against Townsend Spring. He's a horrible cad, as I told you; but I fancy him quite honest. Still, tie's a speculator; he lives on risks and hazards. The market will leave him high and dry, some day; he's bound to be cleaned out, as they phrase it. I'm afraid you don't understand me, because you don't understand Wall Street."

"I understand the keeping of a trust,—not stealing others' money, however a man may make ducks and drakes of his own, said Wainwright, with positiveness.

"True," replied Mr. Binghamton. "Here we are at the club," he continued, as they neared a palatial building, with spacious plate-glass windows and a door-way of imposing grandeur. They soon passed through this entrance, and found themselves in a lofty hall with which two reading-rooms connected, each of noble proportions and splendid upholstery. Wainwright was decidedly impressed. He had seen few clubs in London on a like scale of magnificence. He and Mr. Binghamton presently seated themselves in one of the lordly rooms; they were served by a nimble butler with something to sharpen appetite; a little later they were taken upstairs to dinner in an elevator with seats of crimson velvet and richly gilded panels. The dining-room, situated at the top of the building, was appointed with numerous small tables, nearly all of which were now occupied by members of the club. Silver dishes gleamed against snowy linen; attendants in picturesque livery glided to and fro. The walls were frescoed in some sort of Pompeian arabesque and filigree; the chandeliers were of striking design; everything was on a plan of extreme elegance. When, soon afterward, their dinner was served, Wainwright found it exquisitely palatable.

"I suppose you know nearly everybody here," said Wainwright, observing that his host bowed in several directions.

"Yes, nearly," was the reply. "The Metropolitan has a lot of different sets in it. It's a queer sort of place, this Metropolitan. Not long ago some of the men here got shocked with it because it was so democratic, and organized an infernally select club which they called The Gramercy. But The Gramercy has been a failure. Nobody goes there. Its patrons belong to it, you understand, and that's about all. They damn this, don't you know, but they come here, all the same."

"I should like to have some of your aristocrats pointed out, said Wainwright, with inquisitive composure

Mr. Binghamton took a draught of the excellent claret which his hospitality had supplied, wiped his comic red moustache free of darkening moisture, and looked about the large room with little nervous jerks of the neck.

"I'll do what I can for you" he said, with laughing complaisance. "Upon my word, what an observer you are! If you preserve this inexorable spirit of inquiry you will attain a knowledge of your own country that must do you shining credit."

"I should call it a creditable thing to know one's own country," said Wainwright. As he thus spoke, the words somehow seemed to himself another's, not his. Only a little time ago he would never have thought to frame a sentence with even this moderate glitter of loyalty in it; but now a light stir of the blood went with his speech; it was like a delicate thrill of self-gratulation.

"Do you see that fleshy man with the wide nose and sorrel whiskers? He's one of our governing committee. He has an old Knickerbocker name and a great lot of money. In England he might be a duke, or something in that line. There's very little of him, but he puts on really terrible airs."

"He appears a very gentlemanly person, said Wainwright, with critical deliberation.

"Oh, yes, confound it! That's all he thinks about."

"It is a great deal to think about," said Wainwright, softly. "It is quite a comprehensive idea, if a man chooses to give it full attention. I don't know that it would not last a life-time."

Mr. Binghamton continued his airy specifications. "The short man that our grandee is dining with is a powerful banker. He's not like Bodenstein; he had ancestors that gave tea-parties and stepped through cotillions, fifty years ago, in their prim homes on Bowling Green or along the Battery. Now he's got a palace up the Avenue, and a wife and daughter who rule society."

Wainwright gave his vis-à-vis a surprised look. "Englishman though you are," he said, smiling, "I am afraid that you know more of what New York used to be than I know of what it is."

"It used to be a dreadfully dull place, I suspect," said Mr. Binghamton. "I know an elderly lady who first saw the light in a roomy old house near Washington Square, in the lower part of Fifth Avenue. There were several daughters; they were all beautiful, and had been abroad and got foreign ideas, at a time when foreign ideas were held abominable by your strait-laced progenitors. One day two of them went cantering up the Avenue on horseback, with a mounted groom following. The next day an article appeared in 'The Evening Post,' on the bad taste of certain New Yorkers who aped the manners of London. Wasn't that deliriously provincial?" concluded Mr. Binghamton, looking at his companion over the rim of his wineglass.

Wainwright remembered how Mrs. Spring had anathematized modern New York for this same imitative habit. "I fancy the daily journals would have some hard fighting." he said "if they should wage a similar crusade now a days."

"Aha," laughed Mr. Binghamton, "I suspect that other people than I have been telling you it's the fashion, over here, to reverence the mother country. He suddenly lowered his voice and leaned a little forward. "This young fellow at our right,—

notice him; I mean the one nearest you. You know the other one,—Gansevoort; he was at the Bodensteins' dinner. You remember his name, don't you? Van Horn Vanderventer. His people date back, among your Peter Stuyvesant, days. He and his brother own three solid blocks of houses facing Central Park, besides several empty lots in its near neighborhood. They've been the object of a sort of absurd hereditary conspiracy on the part of several deceased maiden aunts. He's enormously muscular, though he doesn't look it. He spars famously, plays polo, and follows the hounds in a near county, where they actually torture several imported foxes each year, and leap fences on thoroughbreds with all the grand horsemanship of their transpontine cousins. His brother, who is one of the nicest fellows in the world, and a wonderful gentleman besides, drives a coach regularly each day during the milder season, starting from a popular hotel in the city, and carrying passengers several miles beyond the suburban limits. I needn't tell you what that sort of exploit is copied from; you must know all about it, having lived so near the original source of the imitation."

"You are a most capable *cicerone,*" said Wainwright, smiling again. "I think I am very fortunate to have fallen in with you."

"Then there is that lean little man on our left," pursued Mr. Binghamton, in a sort of explanatory carnival. "He's dining with. . . Bless me, if I know whom he *is* dining with! . . . It's some new member or a visitor. . . . I'd surely know him if it were not. He's himself a lawyer, who makes a clean seventy thousand a year. He's splendid company, a great wit, and people break their necks to treat him civilly. . . . Just beyond his table is a fat man with two chins. . . have you got him? Well, he and his wife came from nowhere; but he has a place in the custom-house as fat as himself, and he gives dinners that elevate the soul: the table banked with flowers in January, and a fountain playing in the middle, with a pair of swans floating round in a miniature lake,—actual fact!"

"They must be very well-behaved swans," said Wainwright, dryly. "Prehaps he educates them from the egg up. . . . And now," he continued, with those smooth tones of his, where satire would sometimes sleep like phosphorescence in unstirred water, "pray show me some of your plebeians. Where are they?"

"Don't you see that large round table yonder? There are seven of them dining together,—all Wall Street men. They're mostly very clever fellows, those young stock-brokers; why shouldn't they be? They live by their wits. I don't doubt there are more good things being said at that table than in all the rest of the room. Why, half the wit of the day comes out of Wall Street."

After dining they went down-stairs again, and had their coffee and cigars in the great lower hall. Wainwright soon discovered that his new friend was an extremely popular clubman. Mr. Binghamton left him seated alone for some little time, while shaking hands with this or that friend in the various groups that filled the hall. Occasionally the Englishman would bend down and whisper a sentence in some gentleman's ear, or encircle his neck transiently with one arm, after the most intimate fashion. Mr. Binghamton was evidently at home in all the cliques. Wainwright sat still, drank his coffee, smoked his cigar, and observed. Scarcely a yard from him was a knot of men who had mostly just quitted the dining-room, like himself. Their voices were quite audible to him. One of the group was Mr. Gansevoort; another was the gentleman who had duteously replaced the coal-scuttle at Mrs. Spring's command. Both bowed as they caught Wainwright's eye. Brisk conversation had risen among their companions. Wainwright could scarcely choose but listen to it.

"I'll bet twenty to ten," exclaimed a voice, "that Frank Van Tassell can thrash George Faulkner with the gloves! I've seen Frank spar. He's a devilish tough fellow. Who'll take me?"

"There's not the slightest use of betting," said a second voice. "We can't get up the match. George couldn't be induced to box anybody. He thinks of nothing but dog-fights nowadays."

"I've got a dog," cried a third voice, "that can whip any dog in the United States!"

A general laugh followed these words. Before it ended Mr. Binghamton had again approached Wainwright. "Won't you come upstairs," he said, "and look about a little?"

Wainwright promptly acquiesced. They ascended a broad stairway, entered another Stately hall, and visited two rooms, one devoted to billiards, another to cards. Each was a model of artistic beauty. In each the accommodations for pastime were sumptuously complete. Ebony mantels, velvety carpets, drooping portières, unique frescoes or paperings, combined in the happiest effects of adornment and comfort. Wainwright noted everything with interest, but his mind dwelt sufficiently upon another matter for him to say, during this tour of inspection,—

"I heard a few scraps of conversation among the men with whom Mr. Gansevoort was talking, down in the other hall. The party looked and spoke a good deal in the English manner, but their conversation was extremely muscular. Is it always like that?"

Mr. Binghamton turned quickly, and burst into one of his fresh, light-comedy laughs. "I'm afraid it is," he said. "Those fellows are always talking like a lot of jockeys. They're immensely gentlemanly, however. I suppose their love for all kinds of sporting matters naturally results from their idle lives. They nearly all have large incomes. They are your jeunesse argentée, you know. They have nothing to do except bet and ride and drive their four-in-hands.

"They might find other things to do," said Wainwright. He spoke with a sudden deep seriousness.

Mr. Binghamton's humorous little face lost its smile. "By Jove," he said, "you're right. They might, indeed."

"Could they not go into politics?" asked Wainwright.

"Politics?" repeated his companion. He clapped Wainwright on the shoulder, and laughed again with mud hilarity. "Oh, yes, they could," he said, "but they don't. it you knew more about American politics, perhaps you'd understand why they don't."

Just at this moment Mr. Binghamton and his guest entered the library of the club. It was a chamber appointed with faultless taste; low book-cases were ranged along its crimson walls; every shelf looked well filled. Wainwright stooped and examined some of the books. He found several of his old favorites ready at hand. Taking out one of these, he perceived that its leaves had the stiff crackle of a book which has remained unread. Another volume, and still another, gave the same suggestion of disuse.

He turned toward Mr. Binghamton. "Are these books ever read?" he asked.

"Not often. We have a few men who dip into Thackeray now and then; I suppose on the principle of seeing one's self in the They come here, too, of a morning and skim over the magazines; you see, there's a pile of magazines yonder. But they don't do much solid reading,—bless me, no!"

"You mean at the club? said Wainwright, looking up thoughtfully from a book that he was examining.

"Oh, not a bit of it," said Mr. Binghamton. "I mean at home, abroad, anywhere. Your upper classes here don't read; that's the simple truth. They haven't time; they live in too great a hurry and bustle. One must have leisure, to read; the American knows nothing of leisure."

"The young men have leisure, you say,—those whom I just now heard talking together clown-stairs. Indeed, I can hardly believe that it would not require leisure to assure yourself possessed of a dog which can whip my other in the whole United States."

Mr. Binghamton laughed. 'Oh, those are your rich **young** men; I forgot those."

"Do they form a large class?"

"Rather. It is growing every year."

"And they do not read, either?"

"Dear me, no! Far less even than the fathers who have toiled for years to give them drags and broughams now."

Wainwright seemed to muse for a moment, "They don't read, and they don't take interest in the government of their country?. . . And these are the men who would call themselves our best?. . . It is all very strange to me."

Mr. Binghamton shrugged his shoulders and gave his queer moustache a short tug. "I can't help wondering what you expected to find," said the Englishman, with a keen look from his small hazel eyes.

Wainwright broke into a broad smile. "I expected to find America full of Americans," he said. A moment previously he had replaced on its shelf the book which he had been holding. Directly above him, on the polished top of the low book-case, rested a tome of really cumbrous bulk. He drew it toward him with both hands, intending to read its title. But the cover, loosely detached, came off in his grasp, and several of the leaves fell out on dire disarray.

"Good gracious o exclaimed Wainwright, "what mischief have I been committing?"

"Oh, don't bother about it," said Mr. Binghamton. "That's the British Peerage. I happen to know that the club has ordered a new one."

A curious look had crossed Wainwright's face. He had set his eyes quite fixedly upon Mr. Binghamton. "I thought you told me that they didn't read," he said.

"Oh, bless my soul! they read the Peerage. Why, we wear out a new one every year or so, at the Metropolitan."

"Is it possible?" said Wainwright, dryly.

VII.

At about half past ten, that same evening Mr. Binghamton and Wainwright were driven in a cab to the Grosvenor's ball. It was unfortunate that darkness prevented the latter from taking note of the locality through which their vehicle presently passed, after having clattered through Broadway for some distance, and then threaded a length of most uninteresting side-street. But Binghamton, apt to be an informant no less garrulous than accurate, presently made amends for the disadvantages of the hour.

"We are nearing the quarter in which these Grosvenors live," he said, peering for a moment through the window of the cab. "Notice how broad the street has grown. This is Second Avenue. The especial portion of it through which we are now passing is one of the few fragments of old New York that have still been left uninvaded by a merciless spirit of change. See, . . . here are two parks,—one on either side of us. They are called, respectively, Rutherfurd and Stuyvesant parks. They are full of charming old trees, and neighboring trees have actually been permitted to grow from the centre of the outer sidewalks, as if the pavements had paid a graceful deference to their antiquity. This avenue has something pathetic about it. Years ago your early residents conceived the idea of making it the great opulent thoroughfare that Fifth Avenue is now. Second Avenue ought, indeed, to have been Fifth Avenue. It began with the most brilliant expectations. It lined itself with stately mansions of liberal front; we are passing some of them at present. I can't tell you how many Stuyvesants, Livingstons and Van Rensselaers have lived and died here. A few of them are still living here. But Second Avenue is an embodied disappointment; it is a perished hope. Suddenly the patrician tide set in another direction. A few squares above us the Teutons and Hibernians throng their slatternly tenements. Not far below us the noble old dwellings have been turned into third-rate boarding-houses, where German ladies with big brummagem ear-rings live in splendid usurpation, the wives of prosperous clothiers, tobacconists, or beer-sellers on that horrid adjacent Bowery. But for some little distance Second Avenue still remains (though in a melancholy way) aristocratic. . . . Observe that old church which we are just now passing. You can see it only indistinctly. It is called St. Mark's. It is really a delightful relic. It is hideously ugly, but it has a little space of ground about it which is honeycombed with old family-vaults. I don't know how many deceased grandees sleep there. I shouldn't wonder, my dear Wainwright, if you have some uncles and aunts hidden away in those vaults."

"It is certainly strange to be told this by an Englishman," said Wainwright, quietly, from the darkness. His companion could not see how grave his face looked as he thus spoke.

"We are getting very near the Grosvenors'," pursued Mr. Binghamton, while the cab rolled along. "Do you know, I always have an odd feeling when I come down here to this house? I've lived long enough in New York to have got a certain fondness for it; I detested it at first, but that has quite worn off. The Grosvenors have entertained before. They have lived in their big, dingy mansion for an age. There is an ancient yellow grandmother who does the entertaining. She has two orphaned grandchildren, one of whom has been in society for two years or so, and one of whom is 'brought out' in great state to-night. It seems so strange to meet all the nabobs down here. . . . See the long line of carriages; we shall have to take our turn. A ball up town is different; there it is all brown-stone smartness; it is the natural home of wealth and fashion. But this eastern side of the city is full of want, even squalor. On the pavement where Mrs. Bodenstein will touch her dainty foot as she trips from carriage to doorway, many a weary work-gin has lately dragged her steps homeward. To-night the most imperious creeds of caste and pride will be aired in those perfumed rooms, while perhaps a stone's-throw away, in some plebeian side-street, the O'Flanagans are deep in the mysteries of a 'wake.' I don't think that large, grimy idea called 'the people' ever comes in closer contact with its social opposite, the aristocracy, than when one goes to a ball here in this delightful old avenue."

"Ah," exclaimed Wainwright, "shall I ever grow accustomed to words 'like 'aristocracy' or 'the people,' when spoken under transatlantic skies!"

Mr. Binghamton gave one of his jocund laughs just as their carriage stopped, ready to take its turn in the dark file of others. "My dear Wainwright," he said, "if a man wants to see social distinctions expressed in their most aggravated form, let him come to America to find them."

"I can hardly credit you," was the low reply.

Again Mr. Binghamton laughed. "You haven't met the American element in English life," he said. "You are even more British than I at first suspected of you. I begin to see that you are moderate in everything. You have never moved in those gayer ranks of English society where Americans find such easy ingress. Had you done so you must have seen, long before coming to these shores, how Americans strive and push while in London to gain the heed of titled leaders, how often they succeed, and how both their efforts and their successes prove the absurdly un-republican spirit which tradition has accredited them with."

"I have known only English people in England," said Wainwright.

"As I felt certain," was the quick answer. "Now I took a brief trip to England about a year ago. I fell in with a lot of Americans there,—many of them New Yorkers, whom I had known here. I found that they were mostly having a glorious time. They had got in with Lord This and Lady That. In their own country they were of no social importance whatever; I don't specially know why, but they were not. Having money, expensive habits, and a taste for fashion, they were taken up by a lot of London celebrities. One day I expressed surprise to a fellow-countryman that this condition of affairs should exist. It was no doubt extremely bad taste in me, but I nevertheless committed myself so far. My friend was an enormous potentate; I don't mind telling you who he was,—he was Lord Steeplechaser; I don't doubt you know him."

"Yes," said Wainwright, 'I know him. I don't like his form or his set, but I have met him; and I admit, as you say, that he is a potentate."

"Very well," replied Mr. Binghamton, "this is what he answered me: 'My dear Binghamton,' he said, 'you don't mean to tell me that you have social distinctions over there? I endeavored to persuade him that we had very extreme ones; but he would not believe me. And I suppose you, likewise, will not believe till you see."

"Oh, I have seen," said Wainwright.

"But not enough. You will see more hereafter; it is in the air, as one might say; you are fated to breathe it in. . . . However, my dear fellow, there is one point regarding which I feel a deal of confidence."

"You mean?". . . said Wainwright, in soft interrogation.

"Simply this, responded Mr. Binghamton, leaning sideways, so that some effect of outward lamplight wrought a revealing gleam upon his quaint, small face: "that nothing on earth is easier than for any sort of American, provided he have money and a decent presentability, to get himself recognized in England. Over there they make the same mistake that you make, pardon me, that you made yesterday, and that you will be astonished at having made to-morrow. They assume that everybody over here is of the same pattern. They can't conceive of any differences. Miss Smith, of Topeka, can go to London and be received, if she possess wit, wealth, and good looks. Let her come to New York, and she might languish for years before she got a card to the Bodensteins'—or the Grosvenors', where we are now going. This brings me back to our original subject; I'm such a rambler; I'm always getting away from original subjects. Well, I've only to repeat myself: if you want to see social distinctions more marked than any imposed by the Duke of Belgravia or the Marquis of Mayfair, come to this leading city in the land of liberty, equality, and fraternity, that you may get a good look at them." Here the door of the cab was suddenly opened. "Bless me, it's our turn to get out!" said Mr. Binghamton. "I thought we had a good ten minutes yet, with this crush." And they both got out.

The Grosvenors' house was one of the early products of New York architecture, and its present aged proprietress had always shown the most conservative instincts in its domestic management. She was a little wrinkled old lady, who dressed in scant robes of dark silk and a ruffled cap, after the fashion of fifty years ago, with large gold spectacles crowning her high, shriveled nose, and an antique watch-chain descending from a brooch at the throat. She was in perfect correspondence with the arched, colonial-looking doorway, flanked by narrow side-lights, that led you into her dull yet spacious abode, with its heavy mahogany doors and its slim-banistered staircase; with the straight prevailing stiffness of its furniture and the meagre-rimmed plainness of its mirrors, rising here and there as if in puritan protest against the vanity to which they might minister; with the dark, lofty clock, whose black hands had crept round its brass face for forty years, while its solemn, coffin-shaped case seemed huge enough to accommodate Father Time himself, scythe and all; and with the grim family portraits, mostly in the execrable method of primitive American art. She was a hater of all new ideas, and gossip asserted mat her two grandchildren had pertinaciously struggled before they had broken loose from her rigorous tutelage. But two years ago the eldest of these young girls had conquered restriction and appeared triumphantly in society. The family possessed great wealth, and frequent satire was leveled by their guests at the continued primness of their residence. This was naturally a high source of amusement to those who left Queen Anne mantels smart with blue china, or chambers modishly decorative with Persian rugs and Japanese screens. To-night the Grosvenor mansion, as Wainwright and his new friend presently found, saw its dismal rigidity illumined by a throng of the most brilliant-clad merrymakers. The last inspirations of Parisian millinery inundated these austere rooms in a lavish, rustling over flow. Mrs. Grosvenor stood at the door-way of the front drawing-room, furrowed, decrepit, and like a vivified figure from some portrait on her own walls. Her two grandchildren were close beside her, both of them burdened with a fragrant load of bouquets, one being now the trained society belle, and one having the timid air of the new-fledged débutante. The old lady was extremely deaf, and it was necessary for the eldest Miss Grosvenor to utter very loudly indeed the names of those guests with whom her grandmother was not personally acquainted. She was personally acquainted with very few of the people who were crossing her threshold; she may have been intimate with some of their kindred in remote times, but she had not gone into the social world for at least twenty years, stoutly declaring her entire disapproval of its present reckless expenditures and European innovations, and coldly consenting that a certain family relation, a genial young matron of merry disposition and large acquaintance, should act as chaperone to her recalcitrant grandchild. As the newcomers streamed in, it was worth study to see the quick black eye of Miss Grosvenor first recognize, then beam welcome, and then turn toward her antiquated relative. "Mr. Binghamton, grandmamma," she said, in a loud, assertive voice, as Wainwright and his companion appeared. Mrs. Grosvenor extended a hand to the Englishman, who murmured Wainwright's name a moment later. Miss Grosvenor bowed behind her bouquets; the tyro sister bowed behind her bouquets; then Miss Grosvenor again looked toward her grandmother, but that lady was rather effusively shaking hands with a gentleman whose pink-shining baldness and stooping figure placed him, in all appearance, well among the seventies. Wainwright soon felt his companion gently push him forward, and they were immediately amid the close, babbling multitude beyond. "There's not the slightest necessity of your knowing the old woman," sounded a discreet whisper at Wainwright's ear. "She wouldn't remember your name three minutes, even if she heard it, and she never hears anybody's name; all that is a clever little propitiatory ruse on the part of her granddaughter. Our hostess is the most tiresome old person; she ought to be framed in mahogany and put up in the attic, with her face turned to the wall. . . . If there's anybody here whom you would like to know, my dear Wainwright, command me. . . . Ah, there is Mrs. Spencer Vanderhoff; I told you she would have on the yellow and red sown."

"I think it is quite becoming," said Wainwright. "It gives her an Oriental magnificence."

"Oh, there's nothing barbaric about her," laughed Mr. Binghamton. "She's tremendously civilized."

"I think I should like to know her," said Wainwright. "You say it is fate that I shall, and one had best accept fate philosophically."

When he was presented, a few moments later, to Mrs. Vanderhoff, this lady had just sunk with portly dignity into a chair; two gentlemen were standing near her at the time of Wainwright's introduction, but she broke off conversation with them on the instant, and gave her unshared attention to the new acquaintance. Her face was faded, and yet singularly vivacious; its lines partook of the fleshly fullness that marked her figure, but it still preserved a delicacy that was altered though not spoiled by this matronly change; us expression was richly amiable, as you felt that it must always have been; it was a face that suggested sweet decadence, like the falling apart and curl at the edge in the leaves of a rose too fully blown.

"I am so delighted to meet you, Mr. Wainwright," she said. "I have known a number of your near relations: your uncle, Colonel Wainwright, who brought back such a splendid record from Mexico; . . . your poor, dear mother, who left us and went to England while still so blooming and lovely a widow;. . . your father, whose princely manners won all hearts, and whose sudden death was such a blow to hundreds of his friends; . . . your aunt Gertrude, Mrs. Rivington De Peyster, who was my beloved friend from the days when we were at school together until her death in that beautiful home of hers on the Hudson. Ah, yes, I knew them all! You are so like your mother. . . . I suppose one should not deal in these sad memories at so gay a time as this. . . . But I cannot help it; your face recalls my dear friends to me. . . .

These words were spoken with mellifluous gentleness and an air of fascinating sympathy. One of the gentlemen with whom Mrs. Vanderhoff had been speaking now leaned forward and murmured a few words that compelled her temporary heed. Just then Mr. Binghamton, who had effected the recent introduction and was stationed at Wainwright's elbow, contrived to utter some quick sentences in his ear, covered by a whisper of the most discreet safety.

"She's gushing. She always does, more or less. But it isn't bad fun, sometimes. I don't say she's a humbug, mind, if others do. I think there is a great deal that is real about her. . . . Au revoir,—will try and rejoin you soon."

Mr. Binghamton slipped away. By this time Mrs. Vanderhoff had once more concerned herself exclusively with Wainwright, who now addressed her in his usual suave manner. "Your reminiscences are very far from affecting me sadly," he said. "It is pleasant to be told that I have pitched my tent where I am not of an unknown tribe."

"I trust the stakes are driven in deeply,—are not to be pulled up for a good long while, said Mrs. Vanderhoff, with extreme cordiality.

"I had not thought to stay here long," returned Wainwright. Then he hesitated a moment, before adding, "I had not thought that I should find any reason for staying."

"And you have found a reason?" Here Mrs. Vanderhoff burst into a. soft, full laugh. "Please tell me what it is,—whether its eyes are brown or blue, whether it is short or tall."

"Ah," said Wainwright, "I have not been here long enough to fall in love. I mean the great surprise of it all,' he went on, looking about him, and suddenly lifting both hands. "It is so different from what I expected. True, I should not be able to formulate what my expectations were."

Mrs. Vanderhoff shook one finger at the speaker. Her festal apparel, her mingled repose and sprightliness, the large, imperial grace of her posture, and, more than all, something in her countenance that was fine and suggestive, combined to give her the air of an elderly foreign peeress. Wainwright, as he watched her, could scarcely believe that this grand creature borrowed other people's carriages and opera-boxes.

"I fear that you are ashamed to tell what bad things you expected of us!" she exclaimed, with a delightful smile. "But every day that remain here shall disappoint you more and more agreeably. Oh, yes, I'm convinced of it. I have been abroad, Mr. Wainwright; I have sojourned in nearly all the chief countries of Europe. But it has only made me a devout optimist regarding my own country. We have a great deal to learn, but we know many things that we might teach our wisest contemporaries. Ah, I have an enthusiasm for America, and especially for American women. You have no idea what glorious, lovely beings they are. I know wives, mothers, daughters, here, who are shining models of their sex. They are good and true in such a spontaneous, untrammeled way. They are so much less conscious of their virtue than their sisters across the sea. Often the very acts by which they seem to shock European eyes are the result of a delicious innocence. They are industriously misunderstood by those who have seen womanhood grow up in hot-houses, and not spring with sweet vigor from our new, rich soil."

This may have affected Wainwright as the gush which Mr. Binghamton had cynically prophesied; but in any case it interested him, after the previous exposition which he had gained from a similar source of the lady's rather salient peculiarities. He had already become skeptical of the Englishman's correct judgment. It seemed to him that these candid and fluent expressions were not consistent with the marauding deliberation for which his late companion had so amply prepared him. He began to suspect Mr. Binghamton of being a merciless scandal-monger; he found himself doubting the perpetuity of the red-and-yellow gown, and discrediting the feeble pinkness of the Saturday-evening punches.

"It is very nice to hear any one stand up so valiantly for native institutions, he said. "I have heard no such charitable opinions uttered since my arrival."

"That is because you have seen no one thus far who occupies my point of view as regards American society." Mrs. Vanderhoff spoke these words while crossing her gloved hands in her lap and looking up at Wainwright with a charming seriousness. "I go everywhere; I am in all sets; I observe the whole large social plan, and I assure you it is wonderfully interesting;."

"Mr. Binghamton appears to find it wonderfully cold and formal/' said Wainwright. "Mr. Binghamton sees it with English eyes."

"But he looks upon it from the same com prehensive point of view as yourself," said Wainwright, with sly sarcasm. "I mean that he describes a very extensive orbit. It is parabolic, as the astronomers say."

"Ah, do not speak of Mr. Binghamton as if he were a heavenly body," laughed Mrs. Vanderhoff. "Indeed, he is a most earthly one. He cannot see all our sunshine, nor breathe in all our ozone. He thinks American girls shamefully immoral; he once told me so. Do you know what he bases his theory upon? The harmless flirtations, hand-kerchief-waving, or handkerchief-waving, or hand-kissing, of pert, hoyden-ish little minxes whom one meets on the avenue. That is so like an Englishman! Why, one might as well discover something improper in the frisk of a kitten. Then, too, I don't doubt that the patrician element here seems to him an unwholesome sign."

"It may well seem rather absurd,' said Wainwright.

"It is neither," declared Mrs. Vanderhoff. "It is a splendid protest against the mere vulgarity of republicanism. How monotonous society would be if it were all of a piece, with no 'good,' 'better,' and 'best'!"

"You are truly an optimist," said Wainwright. "You approve of everything."

"I am contented with everything except discontent," smiled Mrs. Vanderhoff, arranging a bit of trimming on her gorgeous gown. "I believe in my surroundings, and I enjoy them. . . . Upon my word," she added, with a still brighter smile, full of something that on childish lips might have been called sweet roguery. "I do not believe there is a woman in all Christendom who enjoys herself more thoroughly than I do!"

"Ah," said Wainwright, "that is because you have the enviable faculty of being easily amused." He was interested, as we know; he regarded Mrs. Vanderhoff, at this moment, in a mood of studious coolness. Whenever she paused he felt toward her as though she were an orchestrion that required a stimulating rearrangement of its mechanism. He had already told himself that she was indeed, in her special way, a type; by no means sure if she were not the most purely American type that he had yet encountered. He could not resist a curiosity to witness, in some manner, the verification of certain hard statements which now rang in his memory with a cruel echo of injustice.

"Easily amused!" replied Mrs. Vanderhoff, with a sort of exclamatory gentleness. "I can find amusement nearly everywhere. I have an abhorrence of loneliness. I like so very much to meet new people; merely to watch new people is a pleasure. I can't ride in a streetcar or an omnibus without finding somebody whom it pleases me simply to watch and speculate upon. I suppose mat is the reason why I rush about so much. I am never bored. There are many people here tonight, men and women, who are constantly bored. They mostly move in one set, and grow weary of the same faces, the same manners, the same rounds of diversion. But I know so many sets; I possess a kind of talisman against *ennui.*"

"Perhaps that is to be explained," said Wainwright, with complimentary nicety, "by your inability to bore other people."

Mrs. Vanderhoff's smile deepened, and she seemed about to reply, when suddenly her hand was extended toward a gentleman who was passing her, and whose shoulder she succeeded in lightly touching. The gentleman turned and made an elaborate bow. As he paused, Mrs. Vanderhoff spoke a few rapid words to him.

"It was so good of you to send me those tickets for the concert, she said, with glowing affability. "I wouldn't have asked you for them if I had not known that you and Madame Francolini were so desperately intimate. Pray tell her for me that she has a charming voice, and that she will never be fully appreciated till she sings in grand opera." Here Mrs. Vanderhoff patted the gentleman's sleeve with the tip of her fan. "Don't let me detain you a moment longer," she said. "I see that Mrs. Effingham is beckoning for you. But thanks,—a thousand thanks."

"The debt is mine," returned the gentleman, nodding and smiling with much geniality as he moved onward. Mrs. Vanderhoff now looked toward Wainwright once more.

"I am afraid that I often bore other people, she said. "But I try to reflect my own good-humor upon everybody. If I fail it isn't my fault. Not to fail, you know, is the secret of not moping through life, devoid of incentive devoid of solace. I have made up my mind to secure both. Don't you think that is a discreet code of philosophy? Come, now, confess that you do."

Before Wainwright could reply to this direct appeal, delivered with a familiarity that was irresistibly winsome, another gentleman had stooped to greet Mrs. Vanderhoff.

"I almost feared that you would not have anything more to do with me," she said, retaining the new-comer's hand a little longer than usage directs, and leaning graciously forward.

"Why not?" replied the person thus addressed.

"Because I must have taxed you so by asking you to do that little favor, returned Mrs. Vanderhoff, deepening her handsome smile. "But you can't think how a ball of that large, public sort charmed my friend from the West. She had never seen anything like it before; it was a precious novelty to her; and I so enjoyed her enjoyment! Of course I could have bought tickets for us both, but then". . .

"Instead of that," was the gentleman's interruption, for which he seemed to have been given just the opportune moment, "you permitted me the pleasure of inviting you both."

Here Mrs. Vanderhoff made some response of which Wainwright could catch but fragmentary sentences. His attention, moreover, was now somewhat distracted by seeing Miss Ruth Cheever pass at rather a distance, upon the arm of a tall gray escort. He saw his chance of departure, and seized it. Mrs. Vanderhoff was sufficiently absorbed, in however transient a way, not to observe the retreat which he now accomplished, with a dexterity born of deft previous practice.

Wainwright had satisfied himself on one point. Scandal had not maligned Mrs. Vanderhoff. Then, too, he had seen Miss Cheever, and wanted, if possible, to secure a talk with her.

VIII.

THE drawing-rooms had now become densely crowded. It was a polite crush. Wainwright found massive trams of silk or velvet obstructing his progress, like headlands to be rounded only with peril. But he had long ago acquired skill and alacrity in this species of locomotion. He perceived that Ruth Cheever had paused near one of the mottled marble pilasters of a mantel not far off; she was smiling somewhat absently as the gray gentleman talked to her. It struck Wainwright that she looked a trine bored, though this pathetic condition was not without becoming results. Her forehead wore the piquant suspicion of a frown; she was biting her nether lip in a fitfully stealthy way notwithstanding her smile, and now and then she would give a nervous, brushing touch with her gloved finger-tips to the bunch of violets worn in her belt. Wainwright saw her face lighten the moment she recognized him. The gray gentleman, who had a very aristocratic way of treating his eyeglasses, and something actually ducal about the lines of his back and shoulders, stared upon Wainwright for a moment, observed the refreshed look of Miss Cheever, and let himself be borne along on the sluggish current of the crowd. He paused, however, before he had gone many yards, and looked back at the two young people whom he had left. Ruth Cheever's strong yet delicate face appeared very animated. The tall, gray gentleman sighed. No one but himself could possibly have heard the sigh, for a band was playing somewhere, and a great buzz of talk mixed with its music. He would not have cared to let the sigh be heard; he might have felt vastly loath to let its cause transpire. He was forty-nine, and a widower with six children. But he was in love with Ruth Cheever, and he wanted very much to marry her. This would make her no less a personage than Mrs. Beekman Amsterdam, sister-in-law of the great Mrs. Bodenstein; and moreover, since he was extremely wealthy, it would make her the mistress of many luxuries and splendors. But Mr. Amsterdam had already offered himself three times to Ruth Cheever, and three times that young lady had refused him. He was considerably discouraged, though not yet quite disheartened. The probability of his asking her a fourth time to be his wife was at present near if not precisely imminent.

"I am very glad to find you here," said Wainwright, as he shook hands with Ruth Cheever. "I had somehow got to fancy that so large a ball would not attract you from home."

"It did not offer striking inducements," she replied, with a weary ring in her voice that had the charm of unconsciousness. And yet I could find no good and just reason for remaining away. It bores me so to think of being bored... but I believe I told you something of that sort before."

Wainwright scanned very steadily the sweet bluish dark of her eyes. "Do you wish to tempt me into a lecture?" he asked. "If so, you will fail. Now that I know you so much better, I think that your peculiar case deserves the most lenient treatment."

She looked at him in genuine surprise. "Pray what has made you know me so much better?"

"Ah, you've no idea how our acquaintance has been progressing since last night. Don't look so incredulous. I assure you, I am very serious. You can't imagine how much I have been thinking about you. We have reached a condition of intimacy that is really extraordinary."

She no longer seemed astonished; she broke into a laugh, and bent her auburn head, touching the knot of violets at her waist with caressing lightness.

"I hope you haven't taken to pitying me, she said, looking up at him with sudden gravity. "I shan't be at all satisfied with your compassion."

"Still, I can't help giving it," he answered, with both the quickness and warmth of impulse. He leaned a little nearer to her as he spoke. "Is your sister here to-night?" he asked.

The color stole rapidly, though rather faintly, into her face. The swift look that she gave him had a vague distress in it, but her slight bitter laugh seemed to express another mood.

"I should not be here if Fanny were not," she said. It struck rum that her tones were now heavy with sarcasm. "My sister has an idea that I am still susceptible of reform,—that I can be moulded into shape."

Wainwright touched her hand; the touch lasted but an instant. He was regarding her very intently. "Tell me," he said, "why you dismissed me so abruptly last night."

She started, and a peculiar expression that lay midway between embarrassment and relief crossed her face.

"I am very glad you spoke of it first," she said. "It had to bespoken of between us,. . . of course."

"I waited for you," said Wainwright, with real tenderness in his moderated voice, "but you seemed averse to begin. If the subject is disagreeable, we will drop it."

Ruth Cheever shook her head in prompt negative. "Oh, no. It is not disagreeable. But I feel that you need no explanation. I feel that you understand the whole state of affairs very clearly. You have convinced me that you are remarkably clever at guessing things."

There was a little pause before he spoke 'It did not require much cleverness, he presently said, "to convince me that your sister is capricious and cruel."

"I suppose that I ought not to let you say that, she murmured, looking down again, while a sensitive quiver stirred her lips. She raised her eyes the next moment: their gaze was calm and direct. "Fanny is very merciless at times," she went on, "and last evening she chose to be specially so. I said, just before you left, that I would explain matters. But really there is not much to explain."

"Then it was only a stratagem to make me go?"

"Yes. . . and no. . . .Well, I will tell you all that need be told. Fanny and I are somehow of a different world. She cannot, or will not, understand me. I don't know that I require much effort for one to understand me. I can be read without the help of a glossary."

"Except when you are willfully misunderstood."

"You are right. I don't know whether you say that only with the pleasant motive of stroking my fur the proper way, or whether there is real sympathy behind your words. But all the same, you are right."

"Now you show a cruel enough doubt to make me remember that you are Mrs. Spring's sister."

"I thought you liked my sister."

"I thought that I did, too," said Wainwright, "though I was not sure about it. Last night made me sure, however. I can't be undecided any longer."

"There is a great deal to like in Fanny. I like her. I love her dearly. I can't help it."

"You are very generous to say so."

"No,—I am not generous. The tie of blood is strong. Besides, Fanny can be kind to those whom she approves of. But she does not approve of me."

"I do not require to be told that. I am afraid that I should fail, if you won her good opinion, to approve of you myself. You decline to whirl through life like a humming-top. You want to sit down on the roadside, now and then, and look about a little."

A spark left the soft eyes that were turned full upon Wainwright's; he hardly knew if it were sad, or merry, or both. "Don't call it a roadside," she said. "The rural metaphor doesn't apply. 'Curb-stone' would be much better."

He laughed gently. "I insist on my own metaphor. She won't let you pick a few wild-flowers occasionally, and look up at the sky. That is how the affair stands between you. Let me be more frank. I am afraid that I tread on thin ice, however; one always does in broaching personalities after a short acquaintance."

"You are changing your ground," said Ruth, with subtle demureness. "I thought you considered our acquaintance already an old one."

"That is encouraging in the last degree," laughed Wainwright. But his face immediately sobered again. "I shall resume my candid attitude," he continued. "You have reminded me of my right to do so."

"Shall your candor take the form of advice?" asked Ruth, neutrally placid.

"No. Only of sympathy. I am afraid to advise you. I should favor a much less tolerant course than the one I have witnessed in you. Perhaps your resignation is better than my hostility would be. Still, there is always something that one ought to weigh well in the idea of making a firm stand against injustice and tyranny."

"I am not resigned," said Ruth. The sparkle in her dark-blue eyes had warmed into brief, keen fire. "Not at all, I assure you," she went on. "But I see the folly of beating against iron bars."

"I should be less philosophic in your case," answered Wainwright, with a sombre setting of the lips. "I should no doubt take the satisfaction of bruising myself recklessly several times."

"Ah," cried the young girl, softly, "that is just the way you learn that your bars *are* iron! No one tamely submits at first, in a case like mine. . . . Fanny is my natural protector,—my only near blood relation. I must live with her; our wise social codes would not let me live alone. She paused now, and knit her forehead a little puzzledly. "You don't know all yet," she went on, in a hesitating way. "You have not learned my sister's chief reason, her giant reason, for disapproving of me."

"I wish you had left that unsaid," he returned, after a slight silence between them.

"It is such an inhuman style of treating a man's human share of curiosity."

She made no response. She was looking past him; he furtively followed her glance, and concluded that he could trace it to no more active object than one of the stiff portraits on the opposite wall. Her face looked thoughtful, preoccupied; he wondered, for an instant, whether she were not reflecting on some extremely decisive reply.

But none came. He gathered boldness, a little later, and spoke with a low ring of feeling in his voice that gave it richness and depth. He was vehemently in earnest, and he wanted so much to make this fact plain beyond all mistake, that for the time he lost heed of his usual deferent nicety, and let his tones verge upon sharp assertiveness.

"I may not know all, as you say. But I know that when I left you last night, at your own request, you were forlornly embarrassed and agitated. And I should like very much to aid you against the infliction of further distress from the same cause. It seems to me a most unhappy and useless thing that you should go on suffering as I saw you suffer then. My acquaintance with your sister is not a new one. I am willing, if you allow, to risk her displeasure by reminding her mat those open jibes and sneers are wretchedly out of taste, apart from any stronger term."

Her dark eyes had widened while she fixed them on his face during this mud but firm outburst. It evidently astonished her, but the recognition of its tender chivalry had clearly appealed to her as well, before Wainwright finished.

"You cannot help me," she said, with a faint quiver in her voice "But you don't know how much I value your wanting to do so." As she went on speaking her tone and manner grew placid again. "Fanny would find an ugly name for your generous intercession; she would visit her wrath on me, as veil. She cannot forgive me for not having just her tastes; we are as opposite as the poles, and that constitutes a sort of impertinence on my part. Believe me, I must bear whatever you saw me bear,—and a great deal more."

Wainwright felt, notwithstanding the kindly spirit in which his own kindness had beer taken, as if a little decree had somehow been passed to the effect that both he and his companion should no longer regard the personal side of the present question. Ruth conveyed this by a delicate access of dignity, which her watcher scarcely knew whether to find in the dulcet compass of her voice, in the deepened droop of an eyelid, or in some closer meeting of the lips. Wainwright was sure that she desired to speak no further of her own domestic troubles. And yet he was himself quite dissatisfied with any such prospective arrangement. He felt profoundly sorry for her, and would have liked if she had handed him, so to speak, each one of her household grievances, that he might make minute examination of its special offense.

"But your sister's principal reason for treating you so ill?" he said. "Am I not to hear that?"

She shook her head. "Not now," she answered, and the reply was tranquilly positive. "Some other time, perhaps; when we know each other better, I mean,—if that time ever comes." . . .

Wainwright was about to respond with a bit of reproach too sincere for so light a name as gallantry, when a gentleman stopped and shook hands with Miss Cheever, and at the same moment Mr. Binghamton touched his shoulder from behind.

"How are you getting on, my dear fellow?" said the Englishman. "Ah, I see, he added, perceiving the young lady who had claimed Wainwright's attention; "you have been in excellent company." Immediately afterward he exchanged a greeting with Mrs. Spring's sister, but at once resumed his low-voiced conversation with Wainwright, while Ruth herself gave heed to the smiling civilities of a young man who had a crisp little crescent of moustache, and who pulled nervously at his watch-chain as though it had some easy mechanical connection with his copious outflow of small-talk.

"Excuse me," continued Mr. Binghamton, in his decorous, neatly-keyed undertone, "but it will only be good form for you to pay court a little to Mrs. Bodenstein, some time before the german begins."

"Certainly, acquiesced Wainwright. "I did not know that she was here. He slipped his arm into Mr. Binghamton s, and made a short, formal bow in the direction of Ruth Cheever, which the profuse courtesies of her new adherent may or may not have permitted her to see. He appeared very willing to accompany Mr. Binghamton. "You shall guide me to Mrs. Bodenstein," he said, as they moved off together. The prevalent confusion of tongues doubtless made his companion unobservant of the indifferent coolness with which be spoke. "You mention Mrs. Bodenstein," he pursued, while they pushed their way through the complex throng, "as though she were indeed a great lady."

"Bless me," said Mr. Binghamton, "she is such a great lady that it's actually amusing. Why, do you know, it went all through these rooms, about ten minutes ago, in a sort of awed murmur, ***Mrs. Bodenstein is here!*** just as if they had said; 'The Queen has arrived!' I wonder what it is that gives that woman such a positively royal prestige."

"Her great wealth, her good descent?" suggested Wainwright, still carelessly.

He was thinking of something else.

"No; not at all. I know plenty of women as wealthy, plenty as well descended. It is not her beauty, either."

"Pray, what is it, then?" asked Wainwright, caring but slightly for the answer, in his present mood.

"Her robust and expansive stupidity. It's her crowning quality. It puts the last touch upon her adaptability as a leader of fashion. If she had been brilliant, or even mildly clever, she would have made enemies. As it is, society has let her slip into its chair of state. She has the grand manner; she is beautiful; she is exceptionally patrician in all ways; and she has no brains at all. I am not sure, by the way, if that isn't her most patrician quality,—to have no brains at all. In any case, she makes the most admirable figure-head that it could have been possible to select."

Wainwright, at this point, grasped his friend's arm with some vigor. "What a charming creature!" he whispered, referring to a young girl directly in front of them.

This young girl was tall and exceedingly sender; she had a radiant face, of the purest pink and white. Her features were cut with faultless exactitude; her head was small, and placed above her long throat and swan-like shoulders with an enchanting grace of poise. She had hair as golden as spun gold itself, and her rounded chin was almost cleft by one deep dimple. She held a mass of bouquets,—violets, roses, lilies-of-the-valley in a somewhat drooping manner, as though the burden weaned her. There was indeed a willowy sort of languor in the girl's attitude; and about her face, notwithstanding its mirth and bloom, hovered an expression of that disdain which comes from the fatigue of conquest. Wainwright felt that with all its beauty it was almost an arrogant face; but he somehow forgave it for being so; its sorcery made even arrogance delightful.

"Ah, you may well ask who she is," replied Mr. Binghamton; and he repeated the young girl's name, which sounded to his hearer remarkably Dutch and quite unfamiliar. "That lovely creature is the great belle of the present season, he continued. "Is she not delicious? Watch how she treats that cluster of men; they are sometimes grateful even for her impertinences. She has made a tremendous success, that girl." Here Wainwright's associate burst out laughing. "By Jove," he proceeded, "what a contrast!. . . Only a yard or two further on stands our friend Miss Spuytenduyvil."

"Yes, I see her."

"Note her mincing, priggish look, as she talks to that spare gentleman with the curved nose. Here is the patrician idea, presented in two opposite aspects. All that's attractive and picturesque in the idea is typified by that popular golden-haired belle; an that's repelling, insolent, and unpalatable about it is to be found in Miss Spuytenduyvil, with her elbows as sharp as her social prejudices and her smiles as sour as her theories. Ah, there's nothing like looking at the same question from two sides. That exquisite damsel makes one think of the Petit Trianon and the Grand Monarque; Miss Spuytenduyvil recalls the Conciergerie, and is a mild justification for the Reign of Terror."

Wainwright laughed; he had begun to draw steady amusement from his new friend's volatile exaggerations and extravagances, where often slept a spark of rare sense, and not seldom of apt wit as well. "To whom is Miss Spuytenduyvil talking?" he asked. He remembered that her present companion was the same tall, gray gentleman whom he had seen in Ruth Cheever's company on first joining her.

"That is Mr. Beekman Amsterdam," was the reply; and then followed a brief but graphic account of the gentleman's high distinction in the way of caste and wealth. "Do you Know," proceeded Mr. Binghamton, "it is a fact that Ruth Cheever has repeatedly refused that considerable personage? See how grim Miss Spuytenduyvil looks; she is his first cousin. I suspect that she is rebuking him for having threatened her with so undesirable a connection.

Wainwright started; the light words chafed him. "Is Miss Cheever undesirable?" he asked. "I should say quite otherwise."

"Oh, my dear fellow. . . . Amsterdam is a perfect fish, of course,—tiresome, bloodless, inane; but then it's widely allowed that Ruth Cheever makes a grand mistake in refusing him. Recollect that horrid brother-in-law, Townsend; think of that vulgar little Lyddy, with Jim Abernethy, a married man, following her about everywhere,—you'll find them in some corner together to-night, I don't doubt at all; and then, Fanny Spring, with so much style that she's bad style, always rushing about so, and not caring a fig for 'tone.' Ah, Ruth Cheever has made a mistake,— depend upon it. One day she'll be sorry. Good heavens! I should think the poor girl would take any chance of getting out of that wretched family. Townsend will smash up, some day; then where will she be? Amsterdam would give her thirty thousand dollars a year just for herself, if she'd take him."

Wainwright was now looking straight at Mr. Amsterdam through a vista of intervening finery and broadcloth. The man had a colorless, ascetic face; he had fixed his dull eye on Miss Spuytenduyvil, who appeared laying down the law to him in her stony, dogmatic way. He had a large cold arch of nose, and a breadth of upper lip so great as to convey the idea that he could at will shroud the whole lower portion of his face under its clean-shorn, capacious expanse.

"Perhaps Mr. Amsterdam means that she small take him, after all," said Wainwright. "The man usually conquers, in such cases," he went on, an unwonted dash of cynicism mingling with his words and manner.

"Oh, Amsterdam will get her," said Mr. Binghamton, off-handedly, "if he only perseveres."

Wainwright turned suddenly toward the speaker. "Do you really believe so?" he said.

"Oh, of course. The pressure is too strong. I don't doubt that the girl abominates him; I should think she might. But then there are the reasons I've already told you of; and besides, her sister, Mrs. Spring, keeps up an incessant persecution; it isn't a constant dropping; it's a sort of steady shower-bath. She thinks it preposterous that Ruth should refuse any such *parti* as Beekman Amsterdam, and tells her so, with varied ornamentations of phraseology, about seven times a week."

"Poor girl!" said Wainwright under his breath. Mr. Binghamton did not hear the comment; it was spoken too low.

IX.

AT this precise period in his experience, Wainwright found himself a prey to diverse bewilderments, as we know; but a definite emotion was also rapidly strengthening within him, like some growth that unfolds with tropic haste. To use a rather cold-blooded phrase, he had been, from the hour of his landing, an admirable subject for impressions. He had crossed the sea with no preconceived opinions; he had lived in that portion of the English world which does most of its thinking after methods that are sometimes moderately European, when not comfortably insular.

His mind was not cobwebbed with any of that gross ignorance regarding our country which it is fair to call by no means a legendary flaw in British civilization. He had no crude expectations of discovering a prairie on the outskirts of New York, or of purchasing cigars from an Indian tobacconist. He had prepared himself, in a rather careless way, to find remarkable things on the other side of the ocean; but his anticipations had been content to deal with the prospect of vast topographical distances, of startling commercial enterprise, and of general precocious prosperity not usually coexistent with a mere century or so of national youth. He had thought very little about the people whom he should find here; he had received no stimulus to exercise his imagination in this respect, for it had been his fate to feel only a sense of dreary drollery when observing certain strangers in London who were pointed out to him as "American." He loved the refinements of life; extreme fastidiousness was the one dominating trait of his temperament; an enemy might sometimes have called him finical or dilettante, though it is doubtful if ever with just reason. In this matter of refinement he had expected nothing from his new surroundings. It was the happy nature of his disappointment, here, that had formed the chief source of his great surprise. But he could not agree with Mrs. Spring that the social picture, as it now met his view, was merely a slavish copy. While a few more days passed he went to a few more entertainments; he began to be convinced that in our mental as in our material atmosphere lay a tingling freshness wholly novel and characteristic. He met quicker wit, prompter decision, less formality of intelligence, less needless deliberation and sobriety. It seemed to him that we drove at a livelier pace than they did in England, but that we avoided quite as many ruts and stones. As a people we fascinated him; he did not like what was coarse about us any better than he liked what was coarse about the country he had just left. Our inconsistencies often amused him as grotesque; our follies and foibles often wore to him a break-neck rashness; our very independence had sometimes a distressing braggadocio. He was perpetually wondering at our restless modes of living, our feverish tendency to annihilate time and to nullify space, our apparent constitutional feud with the idea of leisure. He had repeatedly paused in the midst of a crowded street, and looked about him at what seemed our violent energy of pedestrianism. On one special morning, when a harsh snowfall had been followed by bland sunshine, with the drip of melted icicles from overhead and the retardments of treacherous slush underfoot, this universal bustle and hurry grew doubly notable. The damp, bright languor of the thaw found no analogy among the swift-footed passers, who evaded its glittering water-drops and forded its viscous refuse with unlessened speed. He missed the loitering steps, the ruddy visages, the placid surrender to indolence, which had so long been for him an accepted fact in London thoroughfares. The incessant activity which engirt him at times wore unwholesome suggestions; many of the faces borne past his eye appeared to it pale as though from stress of toil, and sharpened to unwonted leanness by the worry of competitive contest. Again, this same wide evidence of taxed human force touched him with the goad of self-reproach. He felt as if a rebuking mirror were being held up to his own idleness. Nearly everybody about him seemed laboring hard to live; industry, aim, purpose, were everywhere; he caught, in a certain sense, the contagion of thrifty zeal, and yet remained practically a drone amid the eager hive. It vexed him to find so many people struggling to do of to be something important. He was annoyed that fate should have given him nothing that he cared to strive after,—that she should have made him as important as he had any inclination for becoming. When he strolled during a morning into the Metropolitan Club, of which he had been made what is called a six months' visitor, he found there very few loungers like himself; and those whom he did meet began gradually to irritate him as co-victims of an unfortunate prosperity. Their conversation soon proved wearisome; it was usually about horses, and though Wainwright loved to drive or ride a good horse, he objected to making either occupation the sovereign motive of his existence. Among these gentlemen he constantly met Mr. Gansevoort. The latter was always very glad to see him. He was freshly raimented every morning; Wainwright had the fancy that steamers must be continually bringing him new toilets over the water, to judge by the prodigal variety of his costumes. It was diverting, at first, to study the adroitness of his English imitation, and to try and decide just how far it fell short of original models. Mr. Gansevoort walked, talked, sat down, got up, smoked his cigar, and carried his umbrella precisely like an Englishman, and yet the trained vision of Wainwright saw that it was all spurious mannerism, and not unconscious habit. The matter was there, so to speak, but the inspiring soul remained absent. He sometimes, cruelly longed for a chance to let Mr. Gansevoort know that the truth continued patent through all his disguising tact. Once, while seated in the reading-room, intent on a morning paper, he overheard a friend with whom Mr. Gansevoort was talking utter the following sentence, whose tone and manner were not at all according to the British pattern:—

"Well, I had some good sport on that lake last summer. I fished with a pole for three steady hours."

"Ah, yes," said Gansevoort. He had crossed his legs in an attitude of lazy grace; he had on a woolly sack-coat, extremely light in shade, and trousers of such dark hue as to make the contrast especially striking; he also wore gaiters, whose upper portions were of yellowish cloth, and dotted with little pearl buttons. He was smoothing his blond moustache gently with one hand; the other held a half-burnt cigarette. "By Jove," he went on, "it sounds infernally odd, my dear boy, to hear a man talk of fishing with a *pole.* I suppose you mean a rod."

"Oh, well, a rod, if you choose," replied the other, in good-humored conciliation. "Any way, I caught four dozen fine trout."

Mr. Gansevoort laughed. He threw his cigarette among some big logs that crackled in ruddy turmoil under the artistic, tiled mantel. "Upon my word, I beg your pardon, old fellow, he said, with enough politeness to blunt annoyance, "but it always amuses them so on the other side when we speak about *catching* fish. There they don't catch them, you know; they kill them."

Wainwright rose, at this point, abandoning his newspaper. It is true, he had finished a long editorial column on a political subject, and wanted to reflect over it a little. He had of late read a number of similar articles, and found that their substance often demanded considerable reflection. He had begun to be interested as well as confused by transatlantic politics.

In the afternoons, when the club became enlivened by numerous members who had returned from their several "down town" occupations, he would frequently ask, regarding our government, questions in which he was careful to conceal, if possible, the full measure of his regretted ignorance. But the answers which he received struck him, for the most part, as unsatisfactory. They were spoken trippingly on the tongue, and gave no sign that those who made them had paid any thoughtful heed to the vital subjects which they involved. He said one day to Mr. Binghamton,—

"Why is it that the men here don't go into politics?"

The Englishman creased his little tawny forehead, and gave one of his mirthful cackles. "There are too many men who do go, but not half enough gentlemen,—

more 's the pity."

Wainwright looked all about him; he even made a slight, sweeping motion with his hand. The big room was quite populous with members; in the alcoves of three broad windows facing upon Fifth Avenue sat or stood three large groups. "Do you mean," said Wainwright, "that all these men never concern themselves with the politics of their country?"

"Oh, yes," laughed Mr. Binghamton. "They are always very active just before the important elections."

"How?"

"In making bets."

Wainwright was silent for a moment. "And these are our best citizens," he presently said. "I mean, those who have the largest share of wealth, culture, and breeding."

"Take them all in all, yes," answered Mr. Binghamton.

"These are the men who would entertain any great foreign dignitary,—the Prince of Wales, for instance, if he came to our shores?"

Mr. Binghamton nodded. "Some of them did entertain the Prince when he did come," was his reply.

Wainwright said nothing more; but he looked like a man whose thoughts are grave. While he stood with head momentarily drooped, a young man with a very unsuccessful draw' passed him at the side of a friend. "Every body laughed at me," said the young man, "for bringing over so many things. But I find I didn't bring over half enough. One can't really get anything decent to wear here." (The speaker pronounced it "heah.") "Can one?"

The valuable reply to this unpatriotic appeal was lost in distance. But Wainwright had little doubt as to the unqualified nature of its negative. He had already a secure private theory that something very scandalous must be said about America in the Metropolitan Club to elicit a contradictory retort.

As Mrs. Spring had prophesied, he soon found himself the object of much social favor; he was often asked to balls and dinners, and it is safe to say that he was flooded with cards for kettledrums. But contrary to Mrs. Spring's prophecy, on the other hand, he felt himself very far from disliking his new life. More than once he suspected that Mrs. Spencer Vanderhoff had built her rhapsody about American womanhood upon a solid basis of truth. To speak in general terms, most of the women whom he had thus far met since his arrival impressed mm as original, breezy, buoyant, exhilarating. They lacked the winsome constraint of their English sisterhood, and the tender, unconscious prudery which so often, previous to marriage, among the latter, seems to partake of an effect as vernal and poetic as dew on young clover. But Wainwright's vigilant observance had soon discovered that the sea-possession of the American girl, her bold flights of candor, her saucy assaults against conventionalism, and her occasional trick of doing innocent things in a wise and worldly way were all resultant from an educational system where liberty of conduct and purity of motive hold equal control.

For several days after the Grosvenor ball he saw no member of Mrs. Spring's household, with the exception of its master, whom he once or twice met in the great lower hall of the club, at an hour verging upon midnight. Townsend, at these times, had usually just entered, and was on his way up-stairs to the card-room. Wainwright, who seldom played cards, refused, on each occasion, to join him in proposed deeds of hazard. Townsend Spring was profusely cordial, and quite as vulgar as ever. It struck Wainwright that this gentleman presented the most repelling personality that he had yet encountered. He had already learned that Townsend passed among associates for good-natured and harmless, but Wainwright confessed to an uncharitable sensation that his crude faculties, so often dulled with drink, prevented him from being either. He could ill connect a single chivalrous or amiable trait with so much odious coarseness. He had a settled belief in the noble worth of what are called mere manners, and it seemed to him that no one could pass through life at such a clumsy stumble without unconsciously crushing half the fine growths that lay along his path. Townsend always appeared delighted to see Wainwright. He wrung the latter's hand on the occasion of their last meeting, and delivered a sentence in which "devilish glad" and "old boy" were mingled with more heartiness than coherence. Underneath Wainwright's distaste for the man had always lain a secret doubt lest he did him an injustice by so roundly condemning mm. This doubt deepened as Townsend's warm squeeze of the hand tightened, and perhaps put a flavor of new graciousness into Wainwright's manner.

"Fanny was talking about you yesterday," said the husband of Mrs. Spring. "She's going to have a tea-fight in a day or two, and wanted to know where she should send you your ticket. I told her here: that was right, wasn't it? She wanted to give a big dinner-party, instead, but I said I'd be damned if I'd stand the racket." Here Townsend Spring looked at the marble floor with a sort of animal sullenness on his florid face. "Things are getting infernally panicky in the Street,—and there's that wife of mine running up bills at the dressmaker's and flouncing into bric-a-brac shops, just as if I'd made a devil of a strike in something. Tell you what it is, Wainwright, continued the speaker, elliptically, "don't marry. Biggest mistake in the world for a man like you or myself". . . Here Townsend tapped his companion's breast, and men tapped his own, as if to show their complete uniformity of tastes and attributes. "Marriage doesn't help us a bit; it wasn't meant for fellows of our stamp; we. . . we appreciate our liberty, don't you see, and know how to make the most of it."

These later sentences quite destroyed Wainwright's mood of tolerance. He had a sharp realization of how much he really appreciated his liberty, and managed to end the present interview, for that reason, as speedily as possible. There was something about the inclusiveness of Townsend, when referring to "fellows of our stamp," that left a sharp sting; although Wainwright soon charged himself, in amused soliloquy, with egotistic sensitiveness for so often remembering it. But those other words about the household affairs of the Springs—uttered aloud in what their hearer could consider only the most unpardonable violation of all correct and refined feeling—had likewise left their echo in the young man's spirit; and a melancholy echo it was. He could imagine how at least one member of that household must tremble under the shadow of its possible rum, and deplore the reckless, unwifely follies that were bruited abroad, to become the gossip of club-cliques in their leisure for tempting scandals.

If Wainwright had not gone to the Springs since the visit already chronicled, it was not because Ruth Cheever had failed to occupy a good share of his thoughts. It was clear to him that she held a strangely pitiable position in her sister's abode; it was, moreover, clear to him that she was so high-strung and true-fibred as to shrink from having the depth of her wounds even compassionately gazed upon. In thinking afterward of his own proffer to aid her, he had decided that it partook of an almost grotesque quixotism. Her answer had seemed to him both sensible and indulgent; he could not review the matter without concluding that she had given his somewhat unwarranted advances considerably better treatment than they deserved.

The invitation of which Townsend Spring had spoken arrived on the following day. It asked Wainwright's presence at a kettledrum, and in due time he went. He found the upper drawing-rooms of Mrs. Spring's basement-house thronged with guests, who were mostly ladies, and whose conversational clamor, as he crossed the main threshold, produced an effect of hysterical violence. The ladies were all clad in bonnets and walking-suits, excepting Mrs. Spring, who shone resplendent in a costume of varicolored silks; Miss Lydia, whom he afterwards discovered huddled behind the angle of a cabinet, with Mr. Abernethy's olive complexion and black eyes only a few inches from her own pouting, peach-hued face; and Ruth Cheever, darkly attired, composed, exquisitely graceful, and a little paler than when he had last seen her.

"It is a great pleasure to find some one whom I know," he said, pausing at Ruth's side after he had shaken hands with her.

"I am glad to relieve your discomfiture," she replied, smiling. "But I supposed that if you came this afternoon you would know a number of people."

"Pray, why?" asked Wainwright.

"Because you have been going about so much. We seem to have missed each other, but then I have heard of you here, there, and everywhere."

Wainwright laughed. "I didn't know that I left any trail behind me, he said. "I have had so discouraging a time, between ourselves, that I imagined that nobody had given me a thought."

"Oh, you are mistaken there. And why have you had a discouraging time?"

"Disappointment is always slow work, when it is prolonged through a series of evening entertainments and afternoon teas."

"Disappointment?"

"Yes. I have been looking for somebody whom I found it impossible to meet. But at last I have been successful. I feel very much like being congratulated."

She fixed her eyes calmly upon his face. He thought that he had never known till then how blue they were, and yet how shadowy. "Let me congratulate you on your good fortune," she said, with admirable seriousness.

Again he laughed. "Oh, thanks; you needn't. It would sound quite too vain, and

I know you are not that."

Ruth slightly tossed her head. For an instant he almost thought that she was displeased. "I am sure you can't have had a discouraging time," she said, "in your recent social movements. You must have found many chances to enjoy your own talent for saying insincere things handsomely.

Wainwright took a very earnest air. "Upon my word," he declared, "I have wanted exceedingly to have another glimpse of you."

"There was an easy way of securing that.

Just behind Ruth spread a brilliant screen, where orange parrots, haughty in sewing silk, reared their crests against a sky of crimson embroidery. This vivid background gave her figure a sharp relief, clothed as it was in dark, trim vestments, and stole from it new graces of curvilinear litheness. Warm lights broke and changed in her auburn hair, which had been so disposed about her small, charming head as to make a cluster behind of thick rolls and loops, whose density could not hide the wave running through every tress. She had loosely folded her arms, so that they seemed only to rest upon her bosom, and the flowing sleeves that she wore showed their white shapeliness. Her head was thrown slightly sideways; she made a most delightful picture; Wainwright felt as if his pulse quickened a little while he watched her.

"Ah," he said, "you mean that I might have come here. But how could I believe myself welcome after my presence had seemed, that evening, to increase your distress?"

She started, and he saw her mouth grow very grave. "I made a mistake in asking you to go, that night," she said. "You must have thought it strange enough.

"I am afraid you regret dismissing me. That is a dreary reflection, since I took pleasure in befriending you, even with my absence." After a brief pause he went on, lowering his voice. "I sometimes feel as if I had got to know you very well the first time we met, but had been losing ground, so to speak, ever sine."

"This is only the third time. And our surroundings were so different when we first saw each other."

"Yours were most disagreeable," he said. He drew a little nearer to her. "I hope they have altered for the better; and yet that would seem improbable."

"They have not altered for the better," she answered, and he fancied that her lip trembled as her soft, shining eyes sought the floor.

A slight pause followed. "I am very sorry," Wainwright at length said, in a voice that amply indicated his regret. "Does it annoy you to have me speak on this subject?"

She lifted her look quickly. "No. Why do you ask that?"

"You seemed to think me aggressive, at the great ball where we last met. Or did I merely imagine this?"

A sad smile crossed her face and vanished. "Frankly, I thought you a little curious then. But I had given you the right to be. I have thought it all over since, and I feel assured that you were only friendly."

"That is comforting. Such a change of heart reconciles me with having been misapprehended."

Another pause followed between them.

"Won't you have a cup of tea?" Ruth presently asked.

"I don't know why I shouldn't, if you agree to make it for me."

They walked together through the loquacious multitude into a rear apartment. Here was a table loaded with a beaming tea-equipage of silver, and a collection of wide-brimmed porcelain cups, with tiny flowers deftly painted on their brittle frailty. Ruth poured the tea into one of these, clouded its pinkish liquid with a dainty dash of milk, and then poised over the cup a white block of sugar, held between the silver claws of a slender tongs. "Will you take sugar?" she asked.

"Thanks,—just that one lump. I don't usually take it, but this is to be a cup of friendship, I trust, and it ought to be sweetened symbolically. Shan't you join me?"

"Yes," answered Ruth, proceeding to make another cup of tea for herself. "I like a great deal of sugar, so my excess will counteract your deficiency."

Her way of saying these trifles appeared to Wainwright wholly irresistible. The lightsome drollery seemed spiced with actual with because of the fresh smile and playful felicity of gesture that went with it. A little later they had taken two opportunely vacant seats, and were sipping their tea side by side.

"They say tea is unwholesome," said Ruth. "But I always find it wonderfully cheering. Don't you?"

"My own cup certainly cheers," said Wainwright, looking at her with jocose grimness, "but I am afraid that it rather inebriates as well."

X.

WHILE they sat thus together, Wainwright perceived no less a person than Mrs. Spencer Vanderhoff, standing at some distance away, in conversation with two ladies. Mrs. Vanderhoff had to his mind an increased air of distinguished elegance. In her bonnet and her stately street-draperies she had acquired a new majesty. Her animated face, where time had left so mercifully genial an impress, showed her age more as the slant afternoon sun smote it through a near window than when viewed under the mellow flattery of chandeliers. But her undoubted beauty gave this gentle ravage a kind of pleasant pathos there was something tenderly autumnal about it, like one or two russet hints in a green leaf. I am not so great a stranger here, after all," said Wainwright. "There is another person whom I know." And he mentioned Mrs. Vanderhoff's name.

"Oh, of course," laughed his companion. "Who does not know *her?* Not that I wish to breathe a word against her," added Ruth. "You can't think how I admire her,—or how I envy her, too. She so thoroughly enjoys society; she is such a perfect *femme du monde.* It is delightful to watch her. It reminds me of a person taking a salt-water swim. Society refreshes her, makes her tingle. She positively luxuriates in a kettledrum like this. She once told me that it was her habit always to come early on these occasions, so as to get a chat with the hostess."

"She is staying rather late to-day," said Wainwright, as he glanced at his watch.

"That is because she has become absorbed in conversation with that thin little lady. You've no idea how stupid the thin little lady is; but Mrs. Vanderhoff has the art of drawing her out."

"Which will probably be returned to-morrow," said Wainwright, dryly. "The thin lady will draw *her* out,—in the family carriage perhaps."

Ruth burst into a laugh, full of gleeful secrecy. "Then you have heard of. . . of a certain person's peculiarities," she said. "Pray, has she yet asked any service of you?"

"I am requested to take her to an entertainment at Mrs. Cornelia Bateson

Bangs's. Do you know the lady?"

Ruth creased her forehead archly. "I believe she lectures, or something in that way. Mrs. Vanderhoff knows the greatest quantity of people. Everybody interests her. But you must go and pay her your respects. It will only be polite. Remember that you are very conspicuous this afternoon, and very much in demand. I shall be thought almost uncivil for monopolizing you."

"I am afraid that I don't understand," said Wainwright, with a puzzled shake of the head.

"Why, so few gentlemen ever come to kettledrums, you know. They are asked, but they only send pasteboard acknowledgments."

Wainwright let his glance wander through the parted folds of a great velvet curtain. In the room beyond he saw Mrs. Spring; she was talking to three gentlemen at once. She was apparently going through some pantomimic description of a recent experience; both her arms were raised at one moment, with gestures that doubtless imitated a musician playing vociferously upon a brass instrument. The three gentlemen appeared deeply amused; they bent their bodies in laughter during the performance of these jaunty gymnastics.

"Your sister seems to have considerable male society about her just now," said Wainwright.

"All gentlemen like Fanny," said Ruth.

Wainwright leaned a little nearer to his companion. He felt emboldened by something confident and candid in her manner since they had been together this last time. Moreover, he designed to break the ice, if possible, at a single blow, and define to Ruth Cheever just how he wished to stand toward her throughout possible future relations.

"I do not like your sister," he said. He emphasized the pronoun with strength, and he looked at her very steadily.

"You should not tell me so if you do not, she replied, and her voice was low and some what fluttered.

"You mean that it is not good taste?"

"Yes,—I mean that it is not good taste."

"And yet you are not angry with me," he said. His manner was full of soft assertion, but it was extremely respectful besides. "You are not even annoyed. I am sure of it."

"How do you know that?" she asked, slightly frowning, he could not guess whether from pique or perplexity.

He lifted the fragile cup from which he had been drinking, peered within its empty recess for a moment, and smiled very brightly. "I read it here, at the bottom of this cup,—our cup of friendship, remember."

Ruth leaned her head on one hand, looking straight down at the table. She appeared to muse for a brief while. Then she suddenly raised her eyes, and spoke with low speed.

"Fanny left mother and me when she was a mere girl, and came here with her husband. Of course she has made most of her friends through him. I don't like the people whom she likes; I don't like the things that she chooses to do."

"Both her friends and her doings seem rather. . . picturesque," said Wainwright, deliberately loitering a little over the last word.

"Picturesque," repeated Ruth, with an intonation of bitterness. "Yes,—that is precisely what they are. The clique of persons who surround my sister are, for the most part, ignorant,—frightfully ignorant. They never read; they never think; they have a hunger for amusing themselves, and that is about all. They are perpetually getting up things. It is either a dinner-party in a fashionable restaurant, or a driving-party on an English drag, or a supper-party with a german afterward, at which they all romp about like so many schoolchildren. Occasionally they go to the strangest places. Yesterday Fanny lunched with a number of hilarious inmates at Fulton Market, in a common little eating-house, where the oysters are said to be remarkably good. A few nights ago she was one of a party that went and filled two boxes at a big third-rate theatre, where ladies and gentlemen are not supposed to find anything worth hearing or seeing. Last week she made one of another group, who patronized the balcony regions of an enormous beer-garden, off some where in the Bowery, where our lower classes listen to an assemblage of inferior German musicians playing amid odors of bad tobacco. They call this kind of thing a 'lark,' and I am sorry to tell you that their 'larks' are exceedingly numerous. Nearly all the ladies of the set are married,—which is at least a fortunate circumstance. But they are tyrannically cliquish. They have a prodigious idea of themselves. With an absurd sort of sarcasm, they insist upon your being 'somebody' before they will permit you to pass their charmed limits."

"And if you went darting about in this wild fashion," said Wainwright, "I suppose your sister would entirely approve of you."

"Yes," answered Ruth; "that is, provided I"—and then she paused, very abruptly.

"Provided you married to please her, said Wainwright.

"What do you mean?" she asked, quite sharply.

He shrugged his shoulders, and looked impenetrably non-committal. "I suppose she would make your approved marriage," he said, "one of the chief reasons for extending you gracious treatment."

They looked at each other with great intentness for several minutes. It occurred to Wainwright that his face was being scrutinized by a stare of the most pitiless interrogation, and suddenly perceiving the ludicrous side of his own endeavor to appear innocent, tie broke into irrepressible laughter.

Ruth slowly nodded, with an expression of such solemn discovery that it increased his mirth. "What a wretched gossiping world it is!" she murmured.

"Ah, well," said Wainwright, as his laugh quieted, "you can't expect to have grandees laying their fortunes at your feet without also having the world gossip about it."

She was coloring, and the florid progress of her blush along the clear curve of throat and cheek made him regret that it should be so transient.

"I have kept you to myself quite long enough, I fear," she now said, rising, and speaking with thorough ease of manner and no touch of chagrin. "I see that Mrs. Vanderhoff is giving jealous looks in our direction."

"Bother Mrs. Vanderhoff!" said Wainwright, with a covert grimace, rising also.

At this point a suave, precise voice said a few words across Ruth's shoulder, not loud enough for her companion to hear. The latter now perceived that the lean, lofty form of Mr. Beekman Amsterdam had stolen quite near, just as Ruth herself was turning to address that gentleman. He held an eyeglass in the long, white, refined fingers of one hand. He was smiling, and you almost wondered how he could do so and still retain such an amount of cheerless sobriety about his deep, flat upper lip, which seemed stiffly to disapprove of the thin-edged smile beneath it. Wain-

wright drew the conclusion, as he regarded Mr. Amsterdam, that it would be difficult to find a man more perfectly gentlemanly-looking and yet more completely
unattractive. He had never seen stronger outward evidence of a leaden and dismal
personality. It seemed impossible to connect anything like a passion with one who
gave signs of possessing so sluggishly regular a pulse.

Ruth soon afterward made him acquainted with Mr. Amsterdam, who courte-
ously inquired whether he would be among the guests, that evening, at Mrs. Bodenstein's ball.

Wainwright stated his intention of going. "Your sister has been kind enough
to remember me," he added. "I have no doubt that the ball will be one of great elegance."

"There will be a crowd,—a dreadful crowd," said Mr. Amsterdam, giving a
little wave of his upheld eyeglasses, as though he were going to put them on, and
then not doing so. Whenever he had finished a sentence you felt as if something
had been noiselessly closed and a key turned upon it. "But they intend to make it
very pretty, I believe. . . . A lot of flowers, you know, and the picture-gallery open,
of course."

"There will be a gallery of living pictures," said Ruth; "the painted ones will not
receive much attention."

Mr. Amsterdam looked down at Ruth; he had to look down at nearly everybody, he was so tall. "I am sure that you mean to offer the former a contribution,"
he said, and his lifeless eye faintly kindled.

Ruth gave a slight laugh. "Oh, if I did," she replied, "it would not be much
sought after; it would not have a gilded frame." She ended her words in a careless,
random way, turning toward Wainwright.

But Mr. Amsterdam leaned nearer to her. "The frame could not raise its value,
Wainwright heard him say, in swift undertone.

Ruth's attention was now claimed by a small bevy of departing ladies. At the
same moment Wainwright felt a touch on his shoulder, and looking round he perceived Mrs. Spring.

"You must stay and dine with us," said that lady. "Don't attempt to refuse. I
shan't excuse you unless you've a previous engagement. Now look me right straight
in the eyes and say whether you have or no."

"Really," said Wainwright, "you act as if I were prejudiced against dining with you. This is hardly fair, considering that I now encounter my maiden opportunity."

Mrs. Spring had fixed her little black eyes very watchfully on his face. She seemed meditating for an instant; then she started, and came to herself, as it were. "Oh, I suppose you may have no objection to dining here, but you've taken a dislike to *me,* for all that." She nearly closed her eyes, smiled with firm-shut lips, and slowly moved her head from side to side. "I am sure of it; you needn't deny it. I don't see what on earth is the matter."

She suddenly gave Wainwright a sharp tap on the arm with her fan. "We must have a talk about it. The thing will never do, you know, after our desperate intimacy in Switzerland. Yes, we must have a talk. I haven't time now; I must go and attend to people. You'll dine with us at seven o'clock?"

"I shall be most happy," said Wainwright.

"Very well. After dinner you can chat with my sister Ruth, who is *not* going to the Bodensteins' ball, I believe. I shall retire and make my toilette, and you shall tell me how I look, a little later. I take great pride in my new dress; it is handsome enough to be gossiped about in the newspapers. The newspapers gossip about everything, nowadays; but they so often get the descriptions of dresses all wrong. If they make a mistake about my trimmings I think I shall feel like publishing a corrective card, in self-defense. . . . There, good-by! You'll come at half past six, sharp? Don't forget."

Mrs. Spring rustled and tinkled away from him, with short, trotting steps, after having given him another fan-tap on the arm.

Wainwright was not loath to accept her invitation. He slipped from the rooms, a little later, went to his hotel, dressed for the evening, and re-arrived at Mrs. Spring's by the time that she had specified. He found the charming little basement-house emptied of all its gay guests. Ruth was in the reception-room below stairs as he entered this apartment. It struck him that she had a wearied and worried air, though she smiled on meeting him once more.

"I suppose you are prepared for me," he, said, sitting down at her side on the lounge where she was already seated.

"Yes. Fanny told me that you were coming to dine with us."

"You are not going to the ball this evening?"

"No. I have been graciously excused for another night; my sister has let me on. She is so absorbed in the idea of having a particularly delightful time that the result has been a mood of great clemency."

"Tell me," said Wainwright, after a little pause, "do you win no enjoyment whatever from society?"

Ruth shook her head, in slow negative. "No," she answered, as slowly, "it is all very tame to me. I don't deny that the fault is in myself. I don't deny that my vision is perhaps crooked, jaundiced, unfair. But I see nothing except pretension, frivolity and mannerism among the people who make up what is called society. I very often like the way in which they say and do things, but I grow sadly tired of the vacant, aimless things that they say and do."

"You told me the first night I met you that you were by no means a reformer," said Wainwright; "and yet you rarely speak of your contemporaries, of the people among whom fate has thrown you, without making me fancy that you must have some very stringent theories of social reform."

She laughed as he ended, but the laugh sounded to him more like a sigh. She seemed to muse for a moment, and then looked up quickly into his face with the eyes whose dark richness of tint had already begun to haunt his memory when he was away from her.

"I am not a reformer," she said. "I have no distinct theories, though a few decided instincts. I am only a non-conformist,—and sometimes, I fear, rather an ill-tempered one."

Just then Mrs. Spring entered the room. She still wore the same noticeable costume in which Wainwright had last seen her. It was a commingling of silks, each different in hue; it produced a tasteful, harlequin-like effect, striking, though perhaps too violent. Wainwright could not resist the fancy of putting little visionary bells along the edges of each silken segment, and having these jingle instead of her jewelry whenever his hostess moved, after the fashion of a genuine Folly.

Mrs. Spring looked very much out of humor. It was not until Wainwright was seated at the dinner-table with herself, Ruth and Miss Lydia, that the cause of her discontent transpired. The guest had already perceived that she was distressed, and since he had noticed Townsend's absence during the afternoon, and now saw a vacant place opposite Mrs. Spring, the probable cause of this irritated mood suggested itself to him.

"I am having my nerves tried in a most dreadful way," Mrs. Spring suddenly declared. "I am in a frightfully disturbed state of mind.

"I hope your husband is not ill," said Wainwright, tentatively.

Mrs. Spring gave a laugh. "Townsend? Dear me, no! He is as well as ever, I believe. I've not an idea where he is. We're very good friends, Townsend and I, but it can't be said that our acquaintance has yet ripened into intimacy."

As usual with the speaker of these words, their bad taste was not glaringly manliest, from the peculiar trick of *chic* that accompanied their utterance. But Wainwright saw a pained look cross Ruth's face before her sister had finished, while Miss Lydia burst into a short, bubbling laugh immediately afterward.

"No, indeed," continued Mrs. Spring, letting her fork hover over a morsel of fish, which was cooked, like every other detail of the present repast, with savory skill. "My trouble concerns the gross treachery of my dressmaker. I foolishly allowed her to delay sending home my dress for the Bodensteins' ball until the last moment. I have dispatched her three messages to-day, and the dress isn't home yet. I am growing fearfully anxious about it. I can't go if it doesn't come, and I wouldn't miss that ball for anything in the world. I abominate the Bodensteins; they are such horrid snobs that they've always excluded me from their parties before." Here Mrs. Spring shot a rapid look toward her sister. "I don't mind telling you, Mr. Wainwright," she continued, "that Ruth's friend, Mr. Amsterdam, got us invitations for to-night. Half the people who meet me there will suspect the truth, so I have determined to forestall impertinent hints and allusions. They say the house is a perfect palace, and I've a strong curiosity to see it. If that exasperating Ludovici plays me false, I shall revenge myself in some terrible way,—I'm sure I shall."

"Pshaw, Fanny!" here exclaimed Miss Lydia, "you've a lot of other clothes to choose from. I wouldn't care a pin if I were you."

"Lyddy, don't be absurd! retorted her sister-in-law. "I have simply nothing that's fresh, and you know it. That atrocious green and yellow thing that Worth sent me over makes me look an utter fright. I shall never trust Worth again. He has lost all conscience. He seems to think that anything is good enough for America. . . . There's the bell. Hurry, Ellen, and see who it is."

This last remark was addressed with a pronounced gesticulation to the white-capped servant in waiting, who immediately left the room.

"I suppose you are too agitated even to care for sympathy," said Wainwright, choosing this mild sarcasm rather at random.

"You don't say that as if you had much sympathy to offer," returned Mrs. Spring, somewhat tartly. She raised one finger and shook it at Wainwright. "I can't think what has got into you of late. Somebody has been setting you against me, I suspect. I hope it's not Ruth, there. We must have that little talk I spoke of, and find out."

It was impossible to tell whether the crispness that went with these words had its origin in real or mock anger. But the reckless fling at Ruth made Wainwright feel a warmth in his cheek, and sent to his lips a retort that wore an arrow-tip.

"I should have to forego the pleasure of that talk," he said, "if it were to be a question of hearing your sister unjustly accused."

Ruth turned toward him quickly; he saw remonstrance in her look. Just then the servant returned, bearing a note.

"Not my dress!" almost waded Mrs. Spring snatching the note from her who now proffered it. She glanced rapidly at the superscription. "Good heavens!" she began to mutter, breaking open the envelope with fingers that actually trembled. "Suppose she has written to say that my ball-dress . . is". . .

This sentence died away unfinished. Mrs. Spring was staring down at the opened note. She had grown pale, and she looked wofully bewildered. The next instant she rose from the table. "Excuse me," she said, addressing no one in particular; "I am unexpectedly called away—let dinner proceed—I may return before dessert."

She passed with haste from the room. Her words had been flurried, and their tone was almost husky.

"What on earth do you think is the matter?" said Lydia, looking at Ruth with a wide, Childish stare.

"I have no idea," said Ruth, quietly.

The dinner did proceed, and without Mrs. Spring. That lady failed to appear at dessert, and Lydia rose before the coffee was served, declaring that she must go up-stairs and begin her toilette for the ball. She put her head on one side and clasped her plump hands together, after she had risen.

"You haven't any idea how stunning I'm going to look," she said to Wainwright, pausing beside her vacated chair. "I'm going to wear black tulle trimmed with little sun Mowers. Only wait till you see me."

"I small certainly wait," said Wainwright, who had also risen, "provided Miss Cheever will allow of my remaining so long."

"Oh, Ruth will let you stay!" laughed Lydia. She went as far as the door-way with a dancing step, and then abruptly turned, just as she had reached its threshold. She was bad style, as the term runs; her voice and manner were inelegant, and she managed the motions of her full-moulded figure with a sad want of repose. But she was excessively pretty, in spite of this bouncing sort of abandonment, and you felt a sense of playful sincerity when you looked well at her comely, fresh-tinted countenance.

"Ruth will be glad to talk to you for ever so long, I know," she said, with another glance at Wainwright, full of roguish piquancy. "I'm sure she will, She don't like most people, but I'll bet anything she likes talking to you awfully." Lydia then uttered a high trill of laughter, and immediately made a rapid exit.

Wainwright sat down again. The servant was just then handing him his coffee. He bent over the fragrant cup, not looking at Ruth, who sat next him, but saying with pleasant composure, "Miss Spring has a remarkable fund of good spirits."

"Lyddy is a very nice girl," was the prompt answer. "I am very fond of her."

The servant had left them; Ruth had also got her cup of coffee, and was stirring it with a tiny silver spoon. The illumined table stood richly forth from the dark surrounding appointments of the room. A vase of big golden roses and an épergne of costly fruit lifted their soft pomp of color above the crystal array of glasses. The very luxury of the scene brought to Wainwright a sudden distress, as he turned and watched for a moment the light of a chandelier just overhead steal silky glimmers from Ruth's waved hair. It seemed pitiable indeed that this girl, in whom he felt there lay so much that was fine and true, should thus be environed by the chance wealth of a gambling adventurer. A grim thought entered the young man's head as be watched Ruth: he wondered whether the little spoon with which she stirred her coffee and ever been paid for.

"Miss Lydia seems to like you in return, he said.

"Oh, we are the best of friends," answered Ruth, quickly. "I only wish that I"— She paused, biting her up.

"Well," said Wainwright, "what is it.?"

Ruth spoke very seriously and slowly. "I don't mind telling you," she began. Why should I? Everybody knows that Lyddy is receiving the most devoted attentions from a married man."

"Yes, I have heard something of the sort."

"Of course you have heard. If Lyddy were less responsible, less of an overgrown child, I should not care so much. I don't mean that she is of such tender years; it is her mind; mentally, she has always been, and will always remain, a child. You've no idea what a guileless, innocent nature she hides underneath all that slangy crudity."

"And have you never warned her of the peril in which she stands?"

Ruth shook her head regretfully. "What are my warnings worth?" she replied, in placid lamentation. "Fanny is forever turning them to ridicule."

Wainwright seemed to be reflecting. I don't understand," he at length said. "Your sister is careful enough in her own conduct. She leaves a good margin between herself and the edge of any destructive precipice."

"Always," assented Ruth, decisively. "She, who is so guarded and deliberate in all matters where personal discretion becomes needful, shows obtuse folly in the laxity allowed to this poor feather-headed protégée. That is so often true of shrewd people; they surprise us with a stupidity when we least expect it. The day of wrath will come suddenly for poor Lyddy. My sister will wake to a sense of being socially injured. Stern orders will go forth." Ruth lowered her voice, and it was unsteady, as though with feeling, while she spoke the next words. "Then I dread the result. The bridle has lain loose so long on Lyddy's neck And Mr. Abernethy is a man of no principle. His record is a dark one; he is not well received by people of position,— he is simply tolerated. They are waiting for his next escapade, and then, in spite of high connections, he will be mercilessly dropped. At least I have heard all this. I care nothing about it, however; I think only of that poor reckless child."

"Whom you want very much to help," said Wainwright, looking at her with a smile full of sympathetic concern.

"I do!" exclaimed Ruth. She spoke with great fervor, and momentarily laid a hand on his arm. Her tones had a lovely plaintiveness; a new glow broke from her sweet eyes. "I lie awake at night, thinking of some way to drag that unhappy child backward from her own danger."

"Why do you not speak with her? She likes you; she would listen."

"You are right. But Fanny would accuse me of prudish interference." Her voice trembled perceptibly now. "I have enough to contend with from Fanny, as it is. You don't know all. She averted her eyes from his own fixed, interested look. "There is no reason why you should know. I beg you will ask no more,—for the present." She rose speaking in much lighter tones. "Come, let us go into the other room. You may smoke there, if you choose; nobody will mind."

They passed from the dining-room, but had scarcely reached the little apartment near at hand, where Wainwright had first met when a servant appeared, speaking a few words to Ruth in a low voice.

"My sister has been out since we saw her," she now said, rather bewilderedly, "has returned again, and has sent me a message that she wishes to see me at once on some important matter. I can't imagine what it is; perhaps it concerns that mysterious note.". . . Ruth seemed almost addressing her own thoughts, at this point. "Pray, excuse me for a little while, and make yourself comfortable till I return."

"Curiosity always makes me uncomfortable, said Wainwright, laughing, as she left the room. "You have roused mine, though I can't say that is my chief reason for wishing you will not be long away."

He seated himself, after she had gone, in one of the deep, sumptuous armchairs. The soft power of her personality had left echoes behind, that made the silence gently reverberant. She seemed still to be present in a more ethereal way, so unexpected had been hex withdrawal. Wainwright leaned his head on one hand, shading his eyes; he remained thus for some little time. He was having his first experience of a passion. He might not have admitted this there and then; but he admitted that he was profoundly sorry for Ruth Cheever. The girl's position was very clear to him. She had spoken with self-forgetting ardor of Lyddy's danger. To him her own appeared sharply vivid. The boat in which she sailed was going to pieces; that very day he had heard new rumors concerning Townsend Spring's financial ills. Fate had made one of its worst discords in bringing this pure, high-strung creature so near haphazard morality and callous worldliness, but now a black stroke of real tragedy was in the one chance of escape that lay before her. That chance was to marry Beekman Amsterdam. The imagination sometimes puts things very picturesquely to us when it acts under command of the emotions, and it would not be straying far from fact to say that Ruth was now imaged in Wainwright's mind against a background of lurid disaster, where Mr. Amsterdam's unpleasantly tall figure loomed with spectral sharpness.

His rather doleful reverie was ended in the most unforeseen way. He heard a sound of broken voices in the hall outside, two feminine voices, that seemed to clash with each other in excited dispute, yet were not raised much above a whisper. Presently, having risen and given close heed to the sounds, he detected one or two sentences, and was nearly sine that he recognized both voices as well.

"You must not do it!" said the voice which seemed to him Ruth Cheever's.

"I shall!" replied that which he thought to be Mrs. Spring's. "You've no right to try to prevent me. What business is it of yours?"

"You made it my business. You consulted me about it."

"I'm sorry I did. Let me pass, I say, how do you dare act so to me in my own house!"

"I beg of you—come up-stairs for a few minutes—I have more to say to you—Fanny—please do I"—

These latter words were spoken in loud, imploring appeal. Wainwright had no longer the least doubt who spoke them. The next instant Mrs. Spring came hastily into the room. Her face had two deep spots of color. She never expressed the idea of repose, even when most placid. But now there was something electric about her; she looked as if there would be a little spark and a snap if you touched her. For a moment she fixed her small, glittering eyes on Wainwright's face. Then she went back to the half-closed door by which she had entered, and closed it with a slam. After that she came slowly forward again. She had put both hands behind her back, clasping them there, and had drooped her head. When she had got quite near to Wainwright, she raised her head, and he saw that tears were falling from her eyes.

"I have a great favor to ask of you," She said.

XI.

WAINWRIGHT was silent for a short time; possibly surprise kept him so.

"What is your favor, Mrs. Spring?' he men questioned.

"How cold your manner is!" she cried impetuously. She threw herself into a chair, and covered her face for an instant with both hands. Wainwright did not seat himself. He rested an arm on the mantel near which he was standing, and calmly watched her.

Mrs. Spring uncovered her face. As she did so he spoke. Her tears had somehow not touched him. He felt extremely cold toward her. "I am sorry if my manner displeases you," he said. "I have only to repeat my former question."

Mrs. Spring drew out her handkerchief, and pegan to dry her tears. She seemed nerving herself to be composed.

"This is my favor," she presently said, with headlong volubility: "I want you to lend me some money,—a large amount." Then she named the sum that she required. It was indeed large.

Wainwright turned a shade paler. He was thinking of Ruth, and what a wound must have been dealt her pride.

Mrs. Spring did not wait for him to reply. She rose again, and began to speak, rapidly and agitatedly:—

"I know you will think my request more than strange. But my dressmaker, that horrible Ludovici, has just served me the shabbiest of tricks. I had an account with her; it has been running along for several months. Of course it was to have been paid. But she has heard some absurd story of Townsend being in difficulty, and now, at the eleventh hour, the artful wretch springs a trap upon me. She refuses to send my dress for the Bodensteins to-night until I pay her every penny of her bill. Naturally I can't get the amount at such short notice." Here Mrs. Spring paused, evidently controlling a new rush of tears. "True, I might ask some one else to loan me the money," she went on, "but you chanced to be here in the house, and—and—well, I don't feel quite so much shame in coining to you as—as I would in making such a horrid exposé before anybody of my own set, who would bruit the affair all over town to-morrow. I know how good-hearted you are, Clinton Wainwright, and I—I faithfully promise that the money shall be returned as soon"—

The opening of the door which Mrs. Spring had recently closed, cut short her further words. Ruth had entered the room. She was very pale; she looked straight at Wainwright, and immediately spoke.

"I must beg of you," she said, "not to grant what my sister asks."

A sort of white fury dispelled Mrs. Spring's gathering tears. She stared at Ruth for a few seconds, with a curling lip.

"You are making yourself ridiculous," she said, and gave a CJUICK, hoarse laugh.

"I would rather be that than dishonest," replied Ruth. She appeared exceedingly tranquil; her colorless face alone betrayed her feeling.

Mrs. Spring stamped her foot. Even this act was without the vulgarity of mere ordinary rage; it had an audacious grace of its owns, you might have thought it only picturesque in this woman, while in almost any other you would have thought it pitiably out of taste.

"How dare you insult me!" she said to Ruth. "You shall not remain in my house another day. I don't care where you go; you shan't live with me and call me dishonest.

"You have not the money to repay this loan which you ask of Mr. Wainwright," said Ruth, still perfectly calm. "It is dishonest, therefore, to borrow from him."

Mrs. Spring measured her sister with a scornful look. She turned toward Wainwright, while she pointed to Ruth. Her voice had the ring of desperation.

"You have known me much better than you have ever known *her!*" she cried. "Believe her if you choose,—but I don't think you will. I said she had tried to set you against me, and I meant it. She has always opposed and defied me. She owes me everything,—I took her from a country village, and showered advantages on her. But she has always hated me; there was never so unnatural a sister! Even in the matter of marriage she has preferred to injure herself rather than gratify me."

"That does not concern the present affair," broke in Ruth, with weary bitterness, as though brought to face an old detested accusation.

The words seemed only to feed her sister's wrath. "I might not be as wretchedly embarrassed as I am," she exclaimed, "if you had not behaved with such cruel stubbornness. You would marry Beekman Amsterdam tomorrow if you thought it would prove of no benefit to me!"

Wainwright's eyes met Ruth's for an instant. I am very glad that your sister did not marry Mr. Amsterdam, he said to Mrs. Spring, in tones as polite as they were neutrally inexpressive. "If she had done so I could not have the pleasure of accommodating you this evening."

"Do you mean that—you will—lend me the money?" asked Mrs. Spring, moving a step or two nearer Wainwright, with something as eager as greed in her little black eyes.

"I will lend it to you if I can procure it at his hour, he said; "and I think I can."

Mrs. Spring shot a look of triumph toward Ruth.

"My sister cannot return you the money," said the latter, with great firmness. "I feel it my duty to tell you this."

Mrs. Spring burst into a high, nervous laugh. Her excitement seemed almost to have reached the bounds of hysteria. She hurried up to Wainwright and caught his hand between both her own.

"Don't mind what that sly, malicious creature says!" she burst forth. "You are generous and a gentleman. I knew you would do it, I was in such frightful distress. You are so kind and good to offer me help!"

Wainwright looked steadily into her upturned face. "I am helping you in no substantial way," he said. "Do not suppose that I fail to understand this. I am helping you to indulge a whim, a caprice,—nothing more."

"You are giving her what she cannot return," broke in Ruth, at this point. "Her husband has sustained severe losses of late. It is more than doubtful if he ever recovers himself."

Ruth spoke these words with a composure that was almost terrible. To Wainwright she seemed a sort of personified Conscience, lifting itself in serene protest against the falsity and pretension that surrounded her. He felt that she spoke because she must speak, and he knew that in speaking she suffered a deadly mortification.

As he looked at her his heart throbbed faster. He perfectly understood her motive; he clearly realized the noble and womanly impulse that swayed her conduct. More than this, he saw, with intuitive retrospect, how she had suffered and struggled.

He crossed the room with speed, reaching her side. Then he spoke to her, in words too low even for Mrs. Spring's alert ears to overhear. He hardly knew what exact purpose stirred him,—why he had chosen the course which indeed seemed to have set itself before him without any intervention of choice.

"Leave it all to me, he whispered. "I beg that you will say no more. I comprehend thoroughly."

After this he receded several paces from Ruth, again turning toward Mrs. Spring. The latter wore a frown of bewilderment, but her anger had not abated, as her hands, tightly clenched together, showed with distinct effect.

"Oh, she has persuaded you to refuse!" exclaimed Ruth's sister. "Her insolence, her falsehood, has prevailed with you!"

Wainwright took out his watch. "I will endeavor to return in less than an hour, he said to Mrs. Spring. "Will you let me have the address of this person,—the dressmaker?"

Mrs. Spring gave a start. "I have not been disappointed in you!" she once more cried. "You *are* my friend, after all." Then she told Wainwright the required address.

"I think you can trust to me," he said, moving toward the door. "I promise to do all I can for you" He put out his hand involuntarily toward Ruth, as he passed her. She gave him her own hand. It was cold as marble.

Immediately afterward he left the room. A little later he had left the house also.

XII.

IN less than an hour Wainwright returned. As he entered the reception-room he saw Ruth seated there, beside a table on which a lamp was burning under a rose-colored shade. She did not rise as he appeared; her hands were crossed in her lap; her eyes, full of melancholy darkness, slowly lifted themselves to his own. As he drew nearer he perceived that her pallor was still the same, though the lamplight had deceptively tinted it. He sat down at her side.

"Were you expecting me?" he asked.

"You said that you would return, she replied.

"Yes. . . . Your sister has received the dress by this time, has she not?"

"It came about ten minutes ago. A very sad little laugh here left Ruth. "You made quick work of the affair. Expedition in such unpleasant matters ought to be the preferable course."

"It was not so very unpleasant. I had scarcely any trouble to make Madame Ludovici accept my cheque. She seemed to know me,—to have heard of me, or something."

"I don't at all doubt that she knew you by sight, said Ruth, absently, as though not heeding her own words. "She drives in great state, goes to the opera and the theatres, and sometimes, when permitted, peers into doorways and over banisters at entertainments. She is a most frightful snob, and is always trying to have the notabilities pointed out to her."

"Perhaps she thinks me a notability," said Wainwright, laughing. That may account for my smooth sailing into her good graces." He somehow felt that, conversationally, there was frost in the air. He saw that Ruth's manner was preoccupied and despondent. Moved by a sudden access of feeling, he leaned toward her, and placed his hand on the arm of her chair.

"I hope all your distress is now over," he said, with much tenderness. "It is needless for me to assure you of my entire silence. What your sister said was atrocious. I trunk that you were wholly right; I honor you for acting just as you did."

Ruth's answer was choked and uncertain. He could not see her face; she had turned it quite away from him. "Fanny says that I hate her. It is not true. I could not hate her,—though I might have done so if she hadn't been my sister. But it is she who hates me. I would help her even now if I could,—if it were not too late. She says that I can help her still. You know how; she told you."

"Yes, I know now, said Wainwright, very seriously. "But I had heard before she told me."

"Oh, yes," murmured the girl, drearily; "it has been in all the gossips' mouths." He saw her profile, now; it seemed full of pensive firmness. "But I will never do that thing. I would not do it even if it should save Fanny and me from beggary."

"You mean tout you will not marry Mr. Amsterdam?"

Ruth slowly nodded. "Yes, I mean that," she said, under her breath.

"You don't care for him?" questioned Wainwright again.

She abruptly wheeled round in the armchair, spreading out both hands for a moment with a very marked gesture of impatience.

"Ah, what a question!" she softly cried.

"My own impression is that one might as well cherish a sentiment toward a piece of furniture. Still, women are doing this sort of thing every day."

"Thieves crowd our jails, Mr. Wainwright. I don't see why one should steal, on that account."

"Do you believe in marrying only for love?"

"No. For love and respect."

"You seem, however, to have a decided respect for love," said Wainwright, watching the lamplight deepen her pliant hair into warmer auburn.

"I hope I may never lose that," she answered, meeting his look again.

A silence followed. "Twenty years from now," said Wainwright, breaking it, "you may repent this resolve."

"Perhaps. I suppose I shall ossify. Men and women are doing *that* every day,— almost to quote your own words. But I have another reason for refusing Mr. Amsterdam. I would not have told you this, except for what has just happened. Mr. Amsterdam may not be a lovable gentleman, but he is an eminently reputable and honorable one. If I married him I should be forcing him into relationship with a woman whom I am sure that he dislikes, whom he would feel regret at placing among his kindred, and with a man whom I am equally sure that he despises."

Wainwright felt a slight chill creep through him as these words were spoken. They put the speaker beside him in even a more generous and humane light than that in which he had just been observing her. But they somehow put a certain sequence of possibilities in a new light, also. He started noticeably, and scanned Ruth's face with a keen look.

"Good heavens!" he exclaimed. "Do you mean by this that you never intend to marry?"

She broke into as sad a laugh as he had ever heard. "Oh, I have not thought of that," she replied, with faint irony. "I have never considered the question of my marrying,—yes or no."

"I fancy your scruples would vanish if you once fell in love," he said.

"You find them absurd now, no doubt," she returned. "Well, I can't deny that they are, from a worldly point. I have my own sense of right and duty. . . . I grope for the light as best I can."

"I think nothing about you absurd!" exclaimed Wainwright, with vehemence.

"I think you are a very good woman, and I wish more of your sex were like you."

He rose as he spoke, and put out his hand to bid her good-evening. He then saw that a tender surge of color was sweeping over her face.

"Are you going?" she said, rising also, and placing her hand in his.

"Yes. It is just as well for me not to remain until Mrs. Spring reappears. Will you let me come soon again? It shall be only to see you."

"I will let you come as often as you please," she answered, "and I shall be glad if it pleases you to come often." Her embarrassment, which was worn as gracefully as a flower might wear an overburdening weight of rain, gave these words especial charm for their hearer.

He still retained her hand, perhaps a little? against her will. "Pray, tell me" . . . he said. "That harsh threat of your sister's? . . . There is no danger that she will carry it out?"

"She has made it, in her fits of temper, a number of times before. But there is no danger of her turning me out of this house. She would remember, in a cooler mood, that there must be a reckoning between her husband and myself before I quit here for good. You see, I speak quite unreservedly with you. Why should I not, after what has occurred?"

She stood before him, a slenderly beautiful figure, with both hands hanging at her sides, and her face grown pale and tired now that the blush had left it.

"Do you mean that Townsend Spring has embezzled money which you gave him in trust?" asked Wainwright. He almost whispered the words. He wanted to get at the truth, but the truth had such brutality about it that he instinctively spoke it low.

"Yes, I mean that," said Ruth, slowly nodding her head. "I don't hold him as criminal; he took my money and his wife's with good enough intention, no doubt. But Townsend has been a gambler there in Wall Street for ten years. The air he breathes is tainted with temptation. His life is all risk and danger; he is forever fighting chance. One day there was nothing left to fight it with but Fanny's and my money. I don't know if it all went; he has not said so. I suppose he means to die game, as he would call it. But I believe that he *will* die, financially, and with a miserable crash, before many days. I gather this from certain words he has let fall; I have seen him alarmed before, but I have never seen him show despair tin now."

"You should have been harder upon him," said Wainwright. He spoke with excessive solicitude. "My poor girl, you have let yourself be shamefully wronged!"

He saw her chin quiver for an instant. Then she covered her face and sank upon a near lounge, burying her head in one of the cushions. A storm of sobs shook her frame; the tempest had indeed followed the calm. Pierced with pity and surprise, Wainwright stood and watched her. He wondered whether his own commiserating words had thus shattered her tranquillity. In his confusion he could not recall them, but nevertheless blamed himself severely for having uttered them.

Just as he was drawing nearer the lounge—with what consolatory intentions it would be hard to state—Ruth half raised her head, and he caught a momentary glimpse of her face. Tears were streaming from her eyes and bathing her cheeks; her pale mouth twitched once or twice as she strove to speak. She presently did speak, and in gasping, half-coherent tones bade Wainwright leave her. As her head fell forward once more upon the cushion, he slowly receded. Her behest carried with it a pathetic sanctity. . . . He passed from the house a little later. As he set foot upon the lamplit pavements outside, it occurred to him that he was in anything but a mood for the coming ball at Mrs. Bodenstein's. He took a long walk, ruminating upon the strangeness of recent events and haunted by Ruth's wan face and passionate sobs. Circumstance seemed to have replaced the office of time in bringing his acquaintance with this girl to speedy ripeness. He felt that he knew her nature, in its courageous and dutiful simplicity, as well as if they had been friends for years. He thought that she had acted with a purity of motive all the lovelier because it had proved ineffectual. He saw how she had striven against a positive tyranny of misfortune, and that, however this had bent her spirit, its one brave resolve remained unbroken. That last irrepressible outburst had been a weakness that somehow measured her past strength. She would not marry Mr. Amsterdam. He fell to wondering, as he walked onward through the dim city, whether she would have married the man, even if she had really loved him. A. matrimonial connection with the Springs was certainly an odious prospect. It has been said elsewhere in this chronicle that Wainwright was of fastidious temperament. He brought to his mind three images, or rather these images now etched themselves in strong lines of memory upon his consciousness. He saw Mrs. Spring, with her feverish pursuits of pastime, her mettlesome, frivolous, bal masqué manners, and her selfish antagonism against all domestic decorums. He saw Townsend, her husband, treating life like a roulette-board; smoking it up sensually like a quick-consumed cigar; drinking it down, clay after day, like a series of fiery potions; missing all its fine flavors in his greedy, voluptuous haste to gain them; and cutting, as he shambled through his precarious career, a figure little less than socially ribald. And lastly, he saw Lyddy, bouncing, pretty, under-bred, about as dignified as a bacchante, with the taint of commonness in both phrase and demeanor; ignorant that a life-long disgrace threatened, her, and so self-assured, despite all her volatile artlessness, that you marveled if she really had enough innocence left to fail of viewing her folly in its true rash colors.

A sense of these personalities, one after another, slowly visited Wainwright as he moved onward. The result was a vague disheartenment; he could ill account for the feeling. It seemed to follow him with the stealthy pertinacity of one's own shadow. Of what account to him was the whole Spring household? If Mr. Amsterdam had escaped the danger of marrying into it when he lost the happiness of marrying Ruth Cheever, that was quite the patrician widower's own affair.

Eleven o'clock found Wainwright at the Bodensteins' ball. He had finally decided to go, and remain but n brief time. The interest of watching closely for effects of international contrast had somehow fled from him, for tonight at least. He felt that he had had certain graver chords swept with a heavy touch; they still vibrated and tingled. He was in no mood to be played upon by lighter incidents of impression; the treble-allegros would seem trim after the bass adagio.

Nevertheless, the scene about him was of unexpected splendor and beauty. "Say what one pleases," declared Mr. Binghamton, who had found Wainwright in the throng, and had linked arms with him, "there are no such balls in New York as these of Bodenstein's. I don't think that many more brilliant ones are given abroad.

"I don't think so, either," said Wainwright, looking about him.

The immense main hall, with its coil of balustraded staircase, was draped and garlanded with the costliest flowers. Over each doorway, and beneath every chandelier, flowers were also hanging in fragrant, fanciful devices, like bells, crescents, or stars. All the splendor of the various chambers, that glimmered one beyond another in stately perspective, was brightened and enriched by the costumes of the ladies; for they, it would seem, had worn their loveliest attire and donned their choicest jewels, In the great picture-gallery, whose walls were lined with masterpieces of modern art, the youthful portion of the assemblage waltzed to delicious music played by a full orchestra in an overhanging balcony, midway between frescoed ceiling and polished floor. Supper in one apartment still waited unserved, but a glance showed how lavish and commend able were its viands, while the plates from which these would soon be eaten rose in massive piles of silver, and the spoons and forks gleamed beside them, of solid gold. "It always makes me nervous when I have to eat anything here," whispered Mr. Binghamton to Wainwright, as they passed this regal board.

"Why so?" asked his companion.

"I have a dread lest a spoon or a fork should accidentally drop into one of my pockets. It seems like a useless risk of respectability."

Mrs. Bodenstein looked the fit hostess for so grand a festivity. She wore a robe that was a blending of purple velvet and pearly brocade. Her neck and arms were wound about with ropes of diamonds; aigrettes of brilliants flashed in her close-ringleted blond hair like knots of fireflies tangled in a thicket; her dress was literally strewn with large solitaire diamonds, as though some random hand had flung them there, and they had remained, in sparkling adherence. These prodigal adornments only made her rare beauty more manifest; they suggested no ill advised display; she was so exquisite a creature that the glittering tribute harmonized with her own personal radiance, and rivaled but did not outshine it. To-night she was almost wholly speechless; she had ceased even to be commonplace. Several gentlemen stood near her, as if in mute devotion, with their chapeaux-bras held in one hand and their limp gloves grasped unworn in the other, after some recent edict of fashion. A stream of people was constantly passing before the lady through the doorway near which she was stationed, and if her series of incessant bows above the mass of bouquets pressed against her bosom had something of mechanical inanity, it nevertheless justified her statuesque silence, and gave this a sort of magnificent congruity.

Wainwright found a number of ladies whom he knew, and with whom civility forced him to hold conversation. It seemed to him that the imposing character of the ball weighed upon everybody's spirits; or were his own clouded by an unwonted depression? . . . After the supper was served, and the genteel rush of black-coated foragers had in a measure ceased round the bounteous table, he went himself for a morsel or two of the edibles and a glass of wine. Usually moderate in the matter of wine-drinking, his mood tempted him to take more than a single glass. Mr. Bing-hamton joined him, and they once more stood together, convivially sipping the fine, dry champagne, whose foamy supply met the great polite thirst of the guests with magic readiness.

"I'm sure all this satisfies you," said Mr. Binghamton, with a little wave of the hand to left and right, while he held his half-emptied glass a few inches from his short red moustache. "I'm sure you've no fault to find with it all. It's so deucedly refined that even the worst grumbler couldn't critical."

"I am disposed to be critical," said Wainwright, looking about rum for an in-stant. "I am disposed to find a good deal of fault."

'Oh, come, now!" laughed Mr. Binghamton, 'I don't like to hear that from you. I've formed a very high opinion of your taste. I never met a fellow, who had lived abroad for years, with so little bias in his views of things American. You've been wonderfully refreshing to me, my dear boy, after the surfeit I've had of dissatisfied foreigners."

"Oh, I didn't mean to indulge in detracting comparisons," said Wainwright. "Far from it." He took another swallow of wine, with an automatic air and an absent expression; then, setting down his glass, he laid his outstretched forefinger on Mr. Binghamton's coat-sleeve, as men will do when a flavor of admonition lurks in their coming monologues. "I haven't a word to say against the charming way in which all this grandeur is managed," he went on. "I object to it on other grounds. Most probably it is quite as fine a product of civilization as European ball-rooms could furnish, at their best. But there is precisely the point. It is altogether too civilized a product. There is too much of the over-ripe languor about it. It smells of royalty, of imperialism, of anything that is not republican. You would tell me, if I were to ask you, that here are the best people of the land,—those who possess riches and culture most equally combined. But I should like to see the best people of this land less like the slothful aristocracies of others. These splendors do not intoxicate me; they make me think. I ask myself if all history can parallel what I now see. Where has there ever been a country, just one century old, which dared to dream of a haughty plutocracy like this? Rigor, simplicity, and thrift are the milk on which young realms are suckled. We seem to be dangerously unique over here; we are quite without precedents. When other countries have got to be a hundred years of age, their rulers have probably abandoned the habit of breakfasting in a suit of armor, and the defensive soldiery has perhaps been reduced by a few thousands; but I don't believe these gentlemen have given much thought to feasting their friends on champagne and terrapin, or delighting them under canopies of roses. Altogether, we appear to possess a wonderful national newness. With a government that is curiously experimental I find we unite a society that seems already to have hardened and stratified itself, as though it had passed through a dozen developing periods. As I said, it makes one think."

"You began by seriously disapproving," laughed Mr. Binghamton, "and you end by satirizing. I fear that is a proof you are not in earnest."

"I have grown to be very much in earnest," was the reply, "about everything that concerns my country. And I wish that more of the people whom I have met at places like this would but share my sincerity."

Thus far Wainwright had esteemed himself fortunate in seeing nothing of Mrs. Spring; but he was destined soon to meet her, disinclined though he felt for the encounter. She passed him on the arm of a gentleman, within a very short distance of where he stood. He bowed as their glances came together, supposing and expecting that this would be all. But Mrs. Spring had evidently willed otherwise. She came to an abrupt pause, and made a beckoning motion with her fan for Wainwright to approach. This was of course an imperative summons. Just as he had obeyed it she turned to her escort, and requested him to procure her a glass of champagne and water. The gentleman departed, and Mrs. Spring was left temporarily alone with Wainwright.

She was looking extremely handsome. Every trace of agitation had left her face. Nothing but mirthful bloom remained there, and her smile did not at all diminish as she now began speaking, in low, rapid tones. Her dress, rescued under such dramatic circumstances from the clutch of her modiste, was worn with what struck Wainwright as a victorious ***aplomb.*** It seemed to his eye a daring assortment of hues; there was something pyrotechnic about the way in which its reds and golds met without interblending. Still, it had what is called style to a marked degree, and suited the mercurial vivacity of its wearer; we can always tolerate gaudiness in a butterfly.

"I'm having the loveliest time in the world, said Mrs. Spring. "Of course I can't forget that I owe it all to you, dear, kind creature. I'm going now to dance the german. I hope you'll stand near the door of the next room, if you haven't a partner, so I can see you to take you out when my first turn comes. . . . Oh, I forgot; you don't dance, do you? . . . Really, I'm dreadfully ashamed of myself for behaving as I did this evening. I don't mean about the . . . the dress, you know; I mean my rage at Ruth. I suppose she was right, after all. Ruth is a wonderfully conscientious girl. If I don't understand her, I can still respect her. You've no idea how good and sweet she is. I shall have a long talk with her to-morrow. I mean to turn over a new leaf, and treat her charmingly. She's worth a thousand like me. . . . Still, you mustn't think those horrid things she said about poor Townsend's affairs were true. Oh, not at all! She's worried and nervous that he should be in any difficulty. But I've seen him in a worse fix before now. He'll clear himself in a few days; he always does. Still, I forgive Ruth. There isn't a grain of real malice in that girl; it was only her sense of duty; she has such an enormous sense of duty, you know. Of course, it's a splendid thing to have, and I ought to be ashamed ever to find it the least monotonous or tiresome Ruth and I shall begin a grand reconciliation to-morrow; you must come very soon and witness our domestic felicity. . . . And oh, about that . . . little service you did. It shall be all right, you dear boy; don't have the slightest uneasiness. . . . Here comes Mr. Ten Eyck with my champagne, so we mustn't talk state secrets any more.". . .

Wainwright left the ball soon afterward, accompanied by Mr. Binghamton. "Don't think of bidding our hostess good-night," instructed the latter. "Men seldom do it when they leave as early as we are leaving. . . . We'll drop into the club for a few minutes, if you say so. But first I should like to show you a bit of social contrast; I know you relish that sort of thing."

Mr. Binghamton's proffered opportunity was soon made clear. After the troop of urbane footmen had bowed them out of Mrs. Bodenstein's majestic hall, they walked for some little distance through the crisp night-air, and at length came to a dim-lighted awning that extended from the door-way of a certain residence down over its stoop and across the near sidewalk. A number of carriages were grouped close at hand. There had been a similar awning in front of the Bodensteins' house, and a similar collection of carriages. There, as here, a small throng of cabmen had waited on the pavement, and a tall policeman, too, with the usual gilt insignia of buttons and the astral decoration. Thus far it all appeared very much the same to Wainwright as what he had just seen elsewhere. And when he and his companion shortly afterwards found themselves in a drawing-room filled with guests, the resemblance still continued, though lacking that lordly element of space and splendor which belonged to the festival they had just quitted. A compact had been made between Wainwright and his companion that their stay was to be a very brief one. "I don't see by what right you bring me here," he had puzzledly said to Mr. Binghamton. "I understood that cards to balls must always be asked beforehand of the hostess, here as in England."

"Oh, yes, of course they must," said Mr. Binghamton, "as a usual matter. But my friend Mrs. Doughty waives all those rules. Indeed, I doubt if she knows anything about them. I fancy she has only a dim idea that there is any such person as Mrs. Bodenstein, and she will learn nothing of her ball unless she reads of it to-morrow in the 'Times' or 'World.' "

Mr. Binghamton presented Wainwright to their new hostess as "a gentleman from England." Mrs. Doughty was a stout lady, with very beautiful teeth, which her large red-lipped mouth made the agreeable background of one continual smile. She seemed to have a passion for introducing her guests to one another. Wainwright found himself presented to four ladies in about as many minutes. After favoring him with this signal attention, Mrs. Doughty went elsewhere, doubtless to create new acquaintanceships. Wainwright felt grateful when he was enabled to leave the society of a certain young lady who had been last on the list of the four; she called him "sir," and dealt in no conversation except that of acquiescent monosyllables. She had a dull face and very large rosy ears, mat projected them selves hopelessly beyond the reach of artful concealment. This peculiarity, combined with the fact of her silence, gave Wainwright a sort of Darwinian fancy that she had come from a long ancestral line of listeners. The chance of getting away from this unprofitable damsel was given him by the appearance of a lank youth, who approached and diffidently asked her to dance. Wainwright observed that the lank youth was in evening costume, but that his cravat, instead of being the customary hueless cambric, was of violet satin. A little later, however, while standing in a door-way with Mr. Binghamton, he made further observations of a similar sort.

"I begin to see what you meant by showing me a bit of social contrast," he said.

"The young gentleman who just passed us had a shirt-front thickly covered with embroidery; another, who stands yonder by the mantel, wears a white silk, necktie; and here is still another merry-maker, with one of white satin. This at least seems unconventional."

"It might very well strike you as immoral," replied Mr. Binghamton, with a twinkle in his eye, "and I wonder that it doesn't. Let me elucidate a little. You always look so interested when I am elucidating, and I enjoy it so much myself that I believe I was born to be a ***valet de place.*** Mrs. Doughty's friends are all a very colorless lot. They are not snobs not fops: I only wish some of them were; that would give her assemblages a little character, at least. They don't know anything about the Spuytenduyvils, or the Amsterdams, or the Bodensteins,—or even the Springs, for that matter. They are mostly rich, and they hold their heads quite high, I can assure you. Such ghastly deeds as putting on an embroidered shirt, or a white satin necktie, are incidentally committed by their men, as you have noticed, but their women usually dress in the most correct taste. This set has none of the airs and graces of the nabobs. Observe how unceremoniously Mrs. Doughty goes about introducing her gentlemen to her ladies. She never thinks of asking Miss Smith's permission to present Mr. Jones; she presents Mr. Jones, and that is all about it. She's the soul of hospitality, that same Mrs. Doughty. She has none of the grand unconcern we have seen in other hostesses. She really *is* an entertainer; she loves to see her guests happy; it would pain her motherly, kindly heart if she thought any one here was being bored. . . . Confound her!" broke off Mr. Binghamton, in alarmed aside, "I think She's fixed her eye on us. She'll plunge us up to the neck in new introductions. Let's slip away before it is too late."

At the head of Mrs. Doughty's stairs, just as they were descending, wrapped in their great coats, Wainwright and his friend encountered no less a person than Mrs. Spencer Vanderhoff. She had on the scarlet and yellow gown. She looked charmingly fresh, though she had just come from the Bodensteins', and was now about to go down into the drawing-rooms of Mrs. Doughty.

"Do not forget to-morrow evening," she said to Wainwright, in her august yet winsome way. "We are going to Mrs. Bangs's together, and you are to call for me at half past eight. Was not the Bodensteins' ball superb I felt proud to be there." Mrs. Vanderhoff was slowly descending the stairs while she spoke thus, with her head amiably turned sideways, and Wainwright and Mr. Binghamton were follow-ing her. "I told Mr. Bodenstein tonight," she proceeded, "that I considered him a great philanthropist to delight his guests in so refined and delicious a way. I should like to have a medal struck in his honor. His portrait should be on one side and his wife's on the other, with all those glorious jewels about her neck. Don't laugh at me, you skeptical Mr. Binghamton! You never did have any indulgence for my enthusiasms."

"But, my dear lady," exclaimed the Englishman, as they all three reached the lower hall, "you know you have so many enthusiasms!"

"Of course I have," replied Mrs. Vanderhoff, arranging the folds of her dress with one or two stately touches before she entered the drawing-room. "I cultivate them; I pick up all I can find, and I find a great many; there is no monopoly, in this blasé age of ours."

"Don't mind Binghamton," said Wainwright, smiling. "He is only vexed with your enthusiasms because he isn't among them."

"If you side with me in that nice way, returned Mrs. Vanderhoff, nodding to him across her shoulder, "I shall be tempted to put you on the list. . . . By the bye, pray remember that engagement of ours.". . .

"What remarkable freshness that woman has!" said Wainwright to his com-panion, as they quitted the house.

"Oh, yes," agreed Mr. Binghamton, with his short bubble of laughter, "she is amazingly fresh. But she makes society use the watering-pot to keep her so!"

XIII.

THEY went to the Metropolitan Club afterwards, as Mr. Binghamton had sug-gested. Entering one of the spacious rooms on the lower floor, they found a group of members seated together. Otherwise the club seemed quite vacant, though it was presumable that the card-room on the floor above held its usual number of late gamesters. They joined this group, which consisted of gentlemen whom Wain-wright was not specially desirous to meet. He had already seen them all at the Bodensteins'. Mr. Gansevoort was one of them, and the four others were persons of an extreme similarity to Mr. Gansevoort. It was indeed the same group, with one or two variations, whose curiously sportsman-like converse he had overheard on the evening o. his first appearance within the club. The present talk after Wainwright and his companion had seated themselves, was of a character wholly equine. Everybody appeared to disagree with every body else on the subject of certain horses possessed by Mr. Gansevoort himself. The speed, age, and general excellence of these animals had, for some reason, grown a sharp question of debate. Wainwright listened very languidly to the lively defense of their owner, and once or twice felt bored enough to think of departing before the consumption of his cigar. But a little later, after several heavy bets had been exchanged between the disputants, the recent ball became a topic of discussion. Mr. Binghamton, who looked to be on terms of the warmest intimacy with all his surrounders, chose to instigate this change. He informed the company, with impudent good-nature, that they were babbling like a lot of horse-jockeys, and had better find something more sensible to quarrel about. "Why on earth," he finished, addressing Mr. Gansevoort, "did none of you young swells stay later at the Bodensteins'? I supposed you would all remain and dance the german, like respectable supporters of society."

A light, scornful laugh followed these words. It was chiefly delivered by Mr. Gansevoort, but his friends also joined in it.

"An hour and a half at the Bodensteins' was quite enough for me, said that personage, gazing attentively at one of his shoes, and moving his foot to right and left, as though searching for some flaw in its radiance. "I thought the whole affair very vulgar. It is difficult to tell just what it lacked, but it was" . . . (here the speaker paused in his even drawl, and looked directly at Wainwright) . . . "well, I can't say worse than to call it horridly American."

Wainwright felt an irritation prick every nerve. He had been called upon, of late, to hear a good deal of language precisely like this. A few weeks ago he would not have believed that it could ever wound him. He might have realized himself regretting it as a most unpalatable piece of snobbery, but he could not have conceived that it would inflict upon mm any actual grievance.

As Mr. Gansevoort had appealed so clearly to Wainwright, the latter saw fit to answer him. This was done in tones whose dry coolness must have deepened the cut of the words.

"I did not observe, he said, "that the entertainment to-night was peculiarly American. I should have been glad to find it so. Original things are always better man imitations."

Mr. Gansevoort started and stared. If Wainwright's voice had not been so hard, he might have suspected no point of rebuke in what he had just heard, As it was, he slightly colored, and showed a painful uneasiness. Outside his favorite folly he was by no means a bad fellow, of equable temper, courteous instincts, and yet not at all slow to resent an affront. His amiable qualities made him justly popular, and he had many traits of true manliness.

"Our opinions appear to differ," he said, with an accent of satire, entirely forgetting his English intonation. "But I suppose there is no harm in such disagreement, provided it's a civil one on both sides."

Wainwright gave a cold smile. "Oh, certainly not," he replied, "though the best of us are often liable to meet with views that rather try our tempers."

Mr. Gansevoort straightened himself in his chain. "I do not know that I have said any thing to try yours," he retorted, with a distinct frown.

"Frankly, I think you are mistaken, there," asserted Wainwright, raising his voice a little. "I have not seen as much of the country in which I was born as you have done. But I have seen enough to warrant my feeling some resentment toward those who affect the manner of constant idle sneers at her expense. And I consider that the man who enjoys her protection, both as regards life and property, might employ his time more profitably than in pelting her with cheap sarcasms."

Wainwright looked about him at the whole group while he finished speaking. A dead silence followed. He broke its spell by rising, but at the same instant Mr. Gansevoort rose also, and faced him, flushed with anger.

"You are impertinent, sir!" he exclaimed, with blunt heat, and he made a step forward, as though bent upon striking Wainwright. But immediately several forms interposed between the two men. Wainwright found him' self gently but firmly pushed backward by Mr. Binghamton. He was not at all angry; he had spoken with deliberation, and believed, whether rightly or wrongly, that he had administered a most deserved rebuke. Mr. Binghamton and he now walked arm in arm toward the further end of the large apartment, and stood there, holding a low but animated discussion for at least ten minutes. Meanwhile, Mr. Gansevoort, surrounded by his friends, was expressing himself with rather excited gestures, and either receiving the sympathy of those about him or undergoing their efforts at pacification.

Wainwright listened placidly to his friend's suggestion that he should apologize to Mr. Gansevoort. "Of course," said Mr. Binghamton, "the fellow got no more than what he merited. Viewed internationally, he is a donkey. But then comes the unfortunate consideration that there is no law against the existence of that animal. A resigned endurance of nuisances is one of society's harshest rules, but nevertheless you must recollect that you are bound to obey it."

Wainwright smiled during the delivery of this counsel; he did not seem at all displeased with it. But when it was ended, he said,—

"I shall not apologize to Mr. Gansevoort. Ever since I have known him and a number of men who resemble him, they have been straining my patience. To-night he made a ridiculous remark. I replied by a bit of irony that I couldn't resist. It did not then need much to make me speak out the truth, and he used exactly the requisite stimulant. I think that altogether I have let off both him and his little popinjay constituency very easily indeed. I shall remain here a short time longer, and if no new developments occur I shall go home to bed."

Just then a member of the Gansevoort group was seen crossing the room. He presently addressed Wainwright with great politeness. He said that the unpleasant feeling which had recently arisen could no doubt be settled in a friendly way. He thought it quite possible that Mr. Wainwright would admit, on reflection, to having given Mr. Gansevoort good reason for annoyance; and without doubt some message of apology would not, in that case, be difficult of arrangement. This silver-tongued ambassador finished by saying that Mr. Gansevoort felt both wounded and amazed, as he had intentionally given no cause for the rather severe treatment which he had received.

Wainwright heard these diplomatic sentences through, and then tranquilly replied to them.

"I shall offer no apology whatever," he said. "If I told you why, it would doubtless be considered a further rudeness on my part. But I have reasons which seem to me good reasons, and I prefer simply to stand by the opinions which I then expressed."

He bowed to the person whom he had thus answered, and walked with leisurely steps from the room, Mr. Binghamton accompanying him.

"I am afraid there may be trouble about this affair," said the latter, when they had reached the hall. "Gansevoort is furious."

"I don't see how his fury can affect me," replied Wainwright, "unless he should make a personal attack upon me at some time,—which might perhaps be a disastrous step for him to take." He paused, and a chill glitter disturbed his usually gentle eyes. "I may have been wrong, from a certain point of view," he continued. "I can readily under stand just why you think I was wrong. There are often several ways of viewing the same action, and all of them rational ways. But one fact remains: I have resented hearing a great country ridiculed by a small native of it. I have been shocked and disgusted by an arrogant dandy, and I have shown what seems to me admissible displeasure. . . . Shall I say good-night here, or will you go now?"

"I shall remain a little longer," replied Mr. Binghamton, whose gossip-soul doubtless thirsted for the last intelligence from the adjoining chamber.

"Good-night, then," said Wainwright, going into the coat-room to get his wraps. "You know my hotel," he added, laughing, "if anybody should wish to look me up."

"By Jove, I hope it won't come to that!" said Mr. Binghamton, turning away, with one of his droll grimaces.

XIV.

DURING the next day Wainwright received no hostile communication from Mr. Gansevoort, though, judging by what he already knew of this gentleman's contempt for American customs, he would scarcely have been surprised if something as European as a formal challenge had reached him, arranged in punctilious conformity with "the code." While he sat in his room, that afternoon, however, and reflected with soft amusement on the course which it would be best to pursue under circumstances of such grandiose importance, an envelope was brought him from Mrs. Spring. It contained some brief but cordial lines from that lady, and it also contained several bank-notes, each of large amount, whose sum-total fully covered his loan of the previous evening.

This event was a great gratification to Wainwright. It made him feel that his next visit at Mrs. Spring's house would not be paid with any feeling of awkward reluctance. Her late allusions to Ruth had filled him with astonishment. He felt that he had no key to this woman's character. He could not decide whether the change was one of policy or impulse, but he found himself ardently hoping that it would be a permanent change. To think of Ruth now was to waken within him a gnawing anxiety, and as her tragic position had become an almost incessant care to him, the fang of such discomfort was kept rather closely occupied. He resolved to go at once and personally acknowledge the payment of Mrs. Spring's indebtedness. Reaching her house not long afterward, he inquired for "the ladies," and was shown into the small reception-room. Here Ruth soon joined him. She looked even paler and wearier than before. "I have to apologize to you, she said, with a wan smile, when they were both seated. "I behaved so stupidly, so childishly, last night."

"I can't at all agree with you there," said Wainwright, using a sort of kindly decision. "Let us drop that subject, if you please. . . . I have just received a communication from your sister," he went on. "I hope it put her to no inconvenience. Her promptness was quite unnecessary. I suppose you know to what I refer."

"Yes," said Ruth. She looked straight into his eyes for a moment, and something about her worried face suggested to him the reticence and reserve with which she had already met his past efforts to secure her confidence. But this expression was fleeting; if Wainwright had not learned to know her face so well he might not have perceived the subtle alteration. "Fanny procured the money from Townsend; I am nearly sure that she did not tell him for what purpose she required it. But her demand was very imperative. Townsend became enraged, and said many reckless things; they had a miserable scene together; afterward he sent her up the amount from his place of business, with a really terrible little note. . . Oh, dear," she broke off, suddenly, dropping both hands in her lap, and letting them rest there, "it seems so strange for me to be telling you all this!"

"I wish that it seemed quite natural," murmured Wainwright. "I want it to seem so."

Ruth gave a mournful, tremulous laugh. "I have hidden my distress from everybody in such a jealous way till now."

"By everybody you mean the people whom you have met since you came here to live?"

"Yes."

"You told me, the first time I saw you, that you had left some dear friends in that Massachusetts town. It might have comforted you to have spoken to **them** of your sufferings. Why shouldn't you make me a kind of proxy, and act just as if I had known you from childhood?"

"But you don't remind me of those friends at all, said Ruth, shaking her head, with a gleam of tender comedy in her seriousness. "They were very plain and simple people. Some of them write to me now; their letters seem to come from another planet. I often wonder what their counsel would be if I had told them everything."

"You are sure that they would not have counseled you to do one thing: they would not have proposed that you should marry against your will."

Ruth's eyes filled with tears. Her voice shook as she said, "No, no; I am sure they would not. And yet if they knew how my sister had begged and implored that of me his very clay, perhaps". . . She paused; he was resolutely choking back her tears. Wainwright at once spoke, with swift earnestness.

"What do you mean? Your sister has then been so cruel? She assured me last night that she was to treat you with every sign of repentance. Can she have kept her word so ill?"

Ruth seemed bewildered by the force and feeling with which he spoke these words. She was silent for a moment, as if meditating. Then she slowly answered,—

"It was after Townsend had gone, this morning. She made me a passionate, a despairing appeal. Her eyes are open at last: she has seen the truth; it fills her with horror. She is lying in her room now, with a blinding headache. . . . It is very pitiful."

"And you!" exclaimed Wainwright, carried away for the instant by severe indignation. "Can it be possible that the cowardly entreaties of this selfish woman will make you forget the magnitude of such a sacrifice?"

She turned to him with a flushing face. She had apparently caught some of his own eager warmth. "I could never forget that," she broke forth, plaintively. "If I consented, I should know all the time just how hard my task would be!"

"*If* you consented!" cried Wainwright. "But you will not consent!" he hurried on. "You ought not,—you must not!" He had leaned very close to her; his breath swept her cheek. "Tell me," he said,—"tell me that you are still firm!"

Ruth had clasped both her hands tensely together while they still lay in her lap. Again she shook her head; a woful irresolution spoke in this mute act. "Let us say no more about it," she presently faltered, in a dreary voice.

"Which means that you may yield."

The color died from her face while he steadily watched it. She had begun to bite her lips, and he saw her respiration quicken. She had not been looking at him for some moments, but now, as she turned her eyes upon him, they held a feverish light that seemed to have dried their unshed tears.

"What can I do?" she asked him; and her voice was almost a wail, "Fanny says that I hold her life in my hands. You yourself said to me, only a little while ago, that women are selling themselves every day. No one seems to blame them. I suppose it is a very pleasant thing to have your diamonds and your opera-box."

She rose and went to the hearth-place, where a crackling fire had bathed in crimson light the low trellis of polished steel. She placed one foot on the trellis, and stared down into the fire, while its glow made a ruddy breadth of reflection along the front of her dark dress.

Wainwright also rose, and his eyes followed her. He put forward both hands, and held them thus extended for a few seconds. It had flashed upon him that he loved her, and he was indeed on the point of telling her this, and of asking her to become his wife. But presently his arms dropped at his sides. She, meanwhile, had not seen his gesture, nor that he had grown, during this brief time, exceedingly pale.

He went up to her, a little later, and put out his hand. "Good-afternoon," he said. "Give my thanks to your sister."

"Must you go?" said Ruth, placing her hand for a moment in his. "I hope I have not offended you with my worldly views," she continued, while another laugh, short and discordant, left her lips.

He strove to retain her hand, but she drew it away. "Are you going to marry Mr. Amsterdam?" he said.

"I don't know," she responded, looking down again into the red heart of the fire.

"You told me that you would see yourself and your sister beggars rather than marry him."

"I can't deny it. I didn't think, then, what a pressure circumstance can exert. It is crushing me clown, I fear. Oh, we are so often sure of our strength till the time arrives for showing it."

A reproachful answer shaped itself on Wainwright's lips, but it did not find egress. He somehow felt that he had no right to let it pass. A silence ensued. He was looking at Ruth, and she was looking directly down into the vivacious blaze of the fire. He never forgot these few minutes. He never forgot the mental conflict that so memorably weighted them. . .

When, a short time afterward, he was out in the street, walking at rapid pace, he could not recall whether or no he had said good-by a second time. His mood seemed very strange to himself. With enough heat to have kindled a flame of impetuosity, he denounced himself as cold-blooded. He was in love with Ruth Cheever, and he had had the chance of discovering if she would rebuff his open declaration. But a new motive had plucked him by the sleeve, and he had succumbed to its remonstrating whisper. He had thought of forming a hated connection with the Springs, and this thought had made him recoil. Reason seemed winning the day with him against a far less deliberate foe; but while he owned her triumph, he deplored it. He had always told himself that he would marry, if he ever married, as much with his head as with his heart. He had been reared to respect what is termed caste; his peculiar English surroundings, and the stress of early educational maxims, had stamped him with conservatism. But he had felt the force of his century as he grew older, and had watched many green beliefs wither into dry ness, tossing them out of doors and windows so to speak, when they had grown futile en cumbrances. But certain sprays remained; they clung to his mental upholstery, as it were, and scented it with an odor of the past. He wanted his possible wife to bear as white a shield as his own. If he had cast aside all faith in descent and ancestry, as the words are commonly accepted, he still set large store by the truths of heredity. Title and distinction might go for little worth, but it was not so easy to waive the claims of having sprung from an unblemished stock. The influence of these tenets now strongly swayed him. He knew that a passion had risen to do battle with them, and that whichever way the final victory turned, it must leave him some dead to be buried.

Naturally, he was disinclined to keep his engagement with Mrs. Vanderhoff that evening, and once or twice he resolved on framing an excuse for not accompanying her. But in the end he decided that this would be an almost churlish retreat at so late an hour, and determined to face forthcoming events, even though his adverse humor should invest them with a mild martyrdom.

He found Mrs. Vanderhoff bonneted and cloaked, waiting for him to arrive. She gave him a most genial welcome, and as she did so Wainwright could not help catching, beneath the folds of her mantle, a gleam of the inevitable red-and-yellow braveries. They presently left the house together, entering a carriage whose quiet dignities of appointment were visible even in the dim light. Just as a long-coated footman, with massive buttons and cockade, was slamming the door of the vehicle, Mrs. Vanderhoff said to Wainwright, in her blandest manner,—

"This is the carriage of my dear friend, Mrs. Fitzgerald. It is so good of her to loan it me this evening. We are both going afterward to a reception, a late affair, you know,—and she allowed me to make use of it for an hour or two."

"That was very accommodating," said Wainwright.

"Oh, yes. I find that people *are* very accommodating, as a rule. I once heard that an enemy of mine had said I was too fond of asking favors. Upon my word, I don't know but she was right. I am so willing to accommodate other people that I forget, sometimes, their disobliging tendencies. Mind you, I don't say that at all cynically. I am not the least bit of a cynic."

"I know," said Wainwright; "you are an enthusiast. Pray, have you any enthusiasm for this Mrs. Bangs, to whose house we are going?"

"Indeed, yes!" exclaimed Mrs. Vanderhoff. Being seated opposite Wainwright as the carriage rolled along, she leaned toward him in the darkness, and a flash of lamplight showed her white-gloved hands clasped together in momentary fervor. "I think she has a very remarkable mind. I find a great deal in her to enjoy, and in the people whom she has about her, also"

"Tell me," said Wainwright, "do you mix her and her people in with your more conventional friends,—with those who haven't remarkable minds, let us say?"

Mrs. Vanderhoff was silent for a moment, in the darkness. "No," she presently replied, changed, reflective tones. "I have days for each set."

"Oh," said Wainwright, dryly, "you manage it that way."

"Yes. It saves aimless collisions. I like all sorts of people; I can always find something in everybody that amuses, interests me; I am vastly social. But then I recognize the fact that others are not. Imagine Mrs. Bodenstein and Mrs. Lucretia Bangs meeting at the same assemblage! It would be absurd; it would even be melancholy. Mrs. Bangs has produced books, pamphlets, poems, and delivered lectures; I don't believe she has ever written 'woman' for thirty years without employing a capital W. Mrs. Bodenstein,—well, you have met her; you know what she is,—a clear, charming person, and so beautiful, so dainty, so patrician! Each fills her place; each gratifies something in my nature; each is my friend."

"You are very optimistic in your views of society."

"I am very catholic," said Mrs. Vanderhoff, laughing her sweet laugh. "I love to watch humanity in its numberless variations. It is like a delicious panorama to me; it fascinates me. . . . Ah, the carriage is stopping; you will now see something of our literary cliques Mr. Wainwright. You will find them very different from any of the circles in which you have previously moved.". . .

Wainwright had not been five minutes in the parlors of Mrs. Lucretia Bateson Bangs before he was inclined to indorse this criticism. They were small parlors, and they were decidedly crowded. Mrs. Bangs was a lady of great height and angular figure, with gray hair rolled high from an austere, sharp-cut face. Immediately on meeting her, Wainwright found himself presented to a buxom little person, who wore lean, dangling ringlets, but whose face was fat enough for a cherub. This lady was made known to him as Mrs. Eleanor Polhemus Brown, and her hostess pronounced the name with an accent of respectful decision, as though she were dealing in a quotation whose authorship had become classical. Mrs. Brown had on a blue silk dress profusely trimmed along the front with fringes of white bugles, crossing each other in such geometrical precision that the whole embellishment looked like a problem awaiting solution. But there appeared nothing at all problematic about Mrs. Brown herself. She was very easy to solve, Wainwright soon concluded. She spoke with speed and was exceedingly genial. Her rural pronunciations and nasal tones struck him as something most amusingly odd. They indeed almost amounted, in his own opinion, to an actual dialect; he had never heard anything remotely like them before. With more abruptness than their brief acquaintance warranted, he asked the lady whether she was a New Yorker.

"Oh, dear, no," replied Mrs. Brown. "I was born 'n East Rockingham, Vermont. I'm a Green Mountain girl." Here she gave a violent laugh, whose mirth was interfered with by a sudden downward writhe of the lip over her front teeth, two of which were missing. "You're an Englishman, ain't you? No? Mercy! Well, you must 'a lived over there forever and a day. I just adore England m'self! We had to rush things so, though, when we went. 'T was one of Cook's parties, you know. 'T. wa 'n 't nice a bit. But I managed to see everything 't there was to be seen. I always do. I'm a splendid traveler." Wainwright's curiosity was aroused sufficiently for him to feel desirous of discovering whether anybody whose conversation betrayed such slight evidence of culture could be a literary personage. Accordingly he made a bold plunge, and said, with his most courteous manner,—

"I fear that my long residence in England has proved more disastrous to me than I thought, since it has prevented me from meeting with any of your published works."

This was certainly an audacious step; for allowing that he had the right to believe Mrs. Eleanor Polhemus Brown celebrated, from the appreciative solemnity with which Mrs. Bangs had uttered her name, he still had no reason to take for granted, after this daring fashion, the peculiar nature of her renown.

"Oh, my!" exclaimed Mrs. Brown, with another of her resonant laughs, followed by the singular downward drag of the lip, in self-conscious after-thought. "I only write sketches, and things like that; I haven't published any books."

"Ah," said Wainwright, pleased at his triumph, and looking politely interested. "You have then won your present reputation entirely journalism?"

"Oh, yes,—quite so," said Mrs. Brown fumbling with some of her white bugles, in diffident modesty. Her quick tones had lost their impetus. She was less attractive in her present confused state than she had been before it came over her, but there was something so genuine about its very homeliness that Wainwright inwardly blamed himself for having covered her with secret ridicule. "I ain't one of your cultivated writers; I put down my thoughts and feelings just as they come to me, and I s'pose a good deal more feelings come than thoughts. I never knew I could write at all till a few years ago, when I got sending scraps every once in a while to the 'Rockingham Tea-Caddy.' It seems queer to me now, when I think 't I should be a regular contributor, on a weekly salary, to the 'New York Napkin-Ring.'"

Wainwright was about to inquire concerning the character of the journal just named, when Mr. Binghamton suddenly appeared at his side. A gentleman also joined Mrs. Brown, and greeted her. Wainwright observed that this gentleman wore his hair, which was uncommonly long, tossed off his brow in a mane like mass.

"I begin to think that you *are* ubiquitous, he said to the Englishman, as they shook hands.

"What on earth are *you* doing here?" asked Mr. Binghamton, in that remarkable stage-whisper which he somehow contrived to hide away under his stiff little moustache. "Oh, yes, I remember: Mrs. Vanderhoff was to bring you."

"I have met only Mrs. Eleanor Polhemus Brown, as yet," murmured Wainwright.

"I saw you talking with her. I pitied you, my dear boy. I came to your rescue."

"I didn't want to be rescued. I think, her very remarkable. She astonishes me."

"Naturally."

"She appears to be a very sincere person," continued Wainwright. "What there is of her has the ring of truth. But I am amazed that she should be a literary character."

"Oh, by Jove!" muttered Mr. Binghamton, with a surreptitious grimace. "She hasn't a literary hair in her head. You ought to read some of her stun in the 'Weekly'. . . what is it?. . . 'Table-Scraper?' "

"No, Napkin-Ring.' "

"Ah, she has told you about it, has she? It is the worst sort of rubbish. It is supposed to be reformatory and all that. It 'teaches,' you know, and is full of 'cheerful philosophy,' as they call it. And then the writing! Such positively devil-may-care syntax! Verbs that disagree with their substantives in number and person! Adverbs that disqualify verbs, adjectives, and other ad—"

"Stop!" remonstrated Wainwright. "She'll hear you. She has looked this way once or twice already."

"I can't help it," asserted Mr. Binghamton, deep down in his throat. "I must explain her to you. She is such a superb subject for my expository mania. She is the most American of American products. She could not exist anywhere out of this country, and dare to call herself literary. Her popularity with a certain class is unquestionable. But then she has no more business to write than she has to cry and build a house."

Mrs. Brown here turned to Mr. Binghamton, and put out her hand very sociably. "I hope you ain't quite forgotten me," she said, with tier explosive laugh. "I thought I'd just remind you 't we were toler'bly well acquainted, after all."

"Ah, my dear Mrs. Brown," said Mr. Binghamton, with the most courtly bend of his small figure, "I was only watching my opportunity to present myself. And meanwhile I was telling Mr. Wainwright, here, all about how famous you are."

"Oh, good gracious!" exclaimed the lady, with shy exhilaration. "You always were a dreadful humbug. Isn't he a humbug, Mr. Large?"

"I should not like to believe so," said the gentleman with the long hair.

Mr. Large, to whom Wainwright was now introduced, gave mm a vigorous clasp of me hand. He had an athletic frame, a massive head, thick, ruddy features, and shining dark eyes, which he rolled about in a way that bore a sort of leonine correspondence with his copious mane of receding hair. He was per-haps thirty-five years old, though he looked older till you observed the freshness of his coloring.

"Mr. Large is our great coining poet," said Mr. Binghamton to Wainwright, with deferential emphasis. "He is founding a school of his own."

"That is very interesting to Lear," said Wainwright, filling up a pause.

"His poems are perfectly splendid, said Mrs. Brown, with enough gentle rapture to set her slim curls trembling. "I reckon I don't understand them all, though. They're too grand. Some of 'em almost take away a body's breath,—I declare if they don't! They're like a tempest."

"She means in a tea-pot," said Mr. Binghamton to Wainwright, employing one of his adroit guttural asides.

"But then some are *so* hard to understand," continued Mrs. Brown, with a look toward the subject of her eulogy; in which reproach and admiration were coyly mingled.

Mr. Large cleared his throat. It appeared to be a throat that could not undergo this process without a certain magisterial volume of sound resulting from the effort. "I am a pioneer, sir," he said, addressing Wainwright. He put one of his big, well-shaped hands into the front of his close-buttoned coat, holding it there quite concealed, like the celebrated people in antique portraits. "I recognize that there is a great work before me," he continued, "and I am going to do it, if I can, in a manful, earnest, honest way."

Wainwright thought this was a rather impressive mode of beginning to state a case, but he also suspected it to be by no means lacking in self-confidence.

"Mr. Large is writing the poetry of the future," said Mr. Binghamton.

"And pray, what is the poetry of the future?" asked Wainwright, with a civil interrogative smile.

Mr. Large answered the smile with one of gracious commiseration. He again cleared his throat, of which a good deal was revealed to view, lifting its white, solid girth above an expansive turned-down collar and an ample cravat of black silk, worn with loose negligence, as though it had been tied in a strong wind. "The poetry of the future, sir, he replied," is but a name given to that healthy impulse which would sweep away the rhyming pettiness, the sickly and hectic affectation, the absurd metrical restrainments, of the past."

"Mr. Large, you see, tumbles over all the old idols, said Mr. Binghamton to Wainwright. "He doesn't believe in the past at all; do you, Mr. Large?"

There were two little vertical creases above Mr. Binghamton's odd nose, and a kind of quizzical sobriety all over his small, funny face.

"I abhor the past," said Mr. Large. As he spoke he passed one hand along the dense backward flow of his hair, as if to see that it retained the proper picturesque disorder. He would probably have gone on speaking, but just then a young man, who had seated himself at a near piano, began to play, and a universal silence fell upon the company.

The young man at the piano was extremely slender. His locks, which were of a whitish blond, bristled upward from his head, as though some acute galvanic shock had thus disposed them. He played with extraordinary energy, and made the instrument palpitate under the most robust volume of sound. His whole body also palpitated, in rhythmic sympathy with the strains which he evoked. His seat upon the piano-stool appeared to exist under conditions of painful insecurity; one might almost have believed that the surface on which he sat had been heated beyond his powers of composed endurance. As the performance proceeded the frenzy grew more vehement. You would have said that its method involved a destructive motive toward the instrument.

"Isn't it horrible?" asked Mr. Binghamton. in the ear of Wainwright. But I don't know that one caricature is any worse than the other That Large fellow is my special abhorrence He, too, is a distinctively American creation. I don't mean that we haven't vainglorious literary frauds in England, but we can't boast of anything just like him."

"What are his writings like?" inquired Wainwright.

"He calls them democratic chants. They are about boundless prairies and brotherly love and the grand coming amelioration of humanity. They are Carlyle and Emerson jumbled up together in wild parody. He discards rhyme, he discards metre, he insults art. Of course he has a little worshiping constituency; such *poseurs* always do have. They think he is a mighty organ-voice. I wonder why everything that is rhapsodical, incoherent and bombastic is always compared to an oratorio or a church-organ. I advise you to avoid his book. It is printed at the author's expense; its name is 'Earth-Clods and Starbeams.' If that is to be the poetry of the future, Heaven have mercy on our unborn generations!"

Not long afterward the gentleman at the piano ceased his boisterous calisthenics. Another interval of conversation followed, during which Wainwright permitted Mr. Binghamton to take him by the arm and move with him among new groups of guests. They presently met a lady whose name was pronounced to be Mrs. Lucia MacIntosh Briggs,—every lady present appeared endowed with a triple name,— and whose fair, ethereal face expressed the most amiable sweetness. But after exchanging several sentences with her, Wainwright discovered that her responses were framed with great bashfulness and under the most stammering difficulty. No school-girl, fresh from tigid disciplines, could have shown a more distressing embarrassment or a more pitiable uncertainty of phrase.

"She's the cleverest woman in the room," Mr. Binghamton managed to tell Wainwright as the latter turned to him with placid despair.

"You wouldn't believe it, but she is. She can't talk; she can't even think without a pen in her hand. But her tales are fought for by the magazines. She has the most enchanting style,—a simplicity and self-restraint that are phenomenal in this age of gorgeous rhetoric."

A little later Wainwright was made acquainted with a small, nervous, keen-eyed gentleman, who charmed him for some time by a very brilliant now of talk. He had rarely heard a more delicious blending of nimble wit and solid wisdom. He seized the first chance that presented itself of asking Mr. Binghamton whether this nonpareil of conversationalists was also a writer.

"Yes," replied his friend, "and a most miserable one. There you have the antipodes of Mrs. Lucia Macintosh Briggs. Not one of his good things ever by chance gets into his dull, opaque treatises. He thinks he can write,—a delusion from which his friends are sometimes obliged to suffer disastrously. But he can only talk; his pen is a non-conductor."

A very thin young lady, with high cheekbones and a pink spot on each of them, now stood beside the piano, where the bristly-haired young man had again seated himself, and sang to his accompaniment a ballad which had a pretty melody and might have been otherwise agreeable, but for the incessant repetition of the refrain,—"Be still, my throbbing heart, be still!" This tuneful request was made by the songstress with every variety of posture, and in countless different keys. When she had passionately uttered it for the fifth time in rapid succession, and you felt convinced that you were to hear no more of it, she would suddenly moan it forth with pensive andante effect, while her accompanist, who had previously bounced up and down upon his piano-stool with fiery sympathy, would then rise and fall in tender alternations. But at last the voting lady's throbbing heart permanently ceased, and the young man also discontinued his grotesque behavior. Wainwright and Mr. Binghamton now went in search of Mrs. Vanderhoff. They found her in the society of a gentleman who looked about thirty years old, and had a drooping brown moustache which seemed to harmonize with the listless inertia expressed in his tall, relaxed figure and his somnolent blue eyes.

"That is Hilliard, to whom she is talking," said Mr. Binghamton, while they paused near Mrs. Vanderhoff and her present devotee, as yet unobserved by either. "He signs himself T. Rochester Hilliard. He is the sworn enemy of our friend Large. He's a fervent believer in 'art for art's sake', and all that sort of thing. He adores the past just as violently as Mr. Large detests it. He shrinks from science and modern progress as hateful iconoclasts. Didn't you see him shudder just then? He must be talking on those odious subjects. I suspect he has practiced that shudder a good deal at home, before a mirror; I've seen him do it in public on a number of occasions. His verses are so mediæval that you feel, after reading them, as if you had been spending your time in an old bric-a-brac shop. They are full of such words as 'therewithal' and 'alway' and 'peradventure' and 'eftsoons'; they are about ladies with meek handmaidens and trailing draperies and calm eyelids (he is very fond of 'calm eyelids'), who lean out of oriel windows, or else commit indiscretions with lute-playing pages in arrased chambers, while their good lords are fighting the Paynim foe afar. He was born of honest, respectable parents in New Jersey, but he wouldn't write of anything American if you were to offer him the laureateship of the United States. It's astonishing how Large reconciles me to T. Rochester Hilliard, and *vice versa.* I always treat one civilly after I have been talking with the other. They are both such absurd extremists that they react upon one another."

Wainwright laughed. "I never knew you had such a vein of cynicism," he said. "You mustn't think that I swallow half your unmerciful comments on Mrs. Bangs's literary clientèle. I refuse to look at them through your spiteful spectacles."

"Oh, you'll want to borrow my spectacles," retorted Mr. Binghamton, "if you ever under take to read some of their books."

Mrs. Vanderhoff soon afterward discerned Wainwright, and told him that she desired to be taken to her carriage; the hour had no doubt arrived when that vehicle must be returned to its obliging owner. Wainwright and Mr. Binghamton both went with her to the carriage-door, after they had made their adieus to Mrs. Bangs; it had been arranged that they should depart on foot, with their cigars. Mrs. Vanderhoff was in one of her warmest enthusiasms as they bade her farewell.

"I have enjoyed myself so much!" she declared, while bustling down the stoop with her upheld skirts, in dowager fashion. "I always enjoy Mrs. Bangs's evenings. It sharpens one's wits to move among so many intellectual celebrities. And to think that there are people who assert there is no literary society in dear New York!". . .

"I wonder if any gathering of human beings could take place which that extraordinary woman would not enjoy," said Mr. Binghamton, as he and Wainwright walked onward, after Mrs. Vanderhoff had been borne away in her friend's elegant equipage. "By the bye, my dear fellow," he presently continued, breaking a brief silence, "you haven't asked me about the result of that affair last night at the club."

"I had forgotten to ask you," returned Wainwright, carelessly enough.

"The matter is making a great stir."

"You don't tell me? Shall I be ostracized among the upper circles? Or shall I be challenged to mortal combat?"

"Neither. You will find some adherents and some detractors. Already people are arraying themselves for and against your cause. The admirers of Gansevoort think you behaved shockingly. His enemies—or rather those who have suffered from a certain arrogance which he sometimes shows toward persons whom he dislikes—applaud your course, and say that you ought to be thanked for putting down an offensive snob. Of course Gansevoort and the small clique who witnessed the affair vent their spleen in hard terms. There was actually a little talk of a challenge last night, after you left. But that blew over, necessarily."

The two men walked on in silence for a few moments. Mr. Binghamton was evidently waiting for some answer from Wainwright which should bear upon the subject that he had broached; but presently his companion rather surprised him by saying,—

"Tell me, Binghamton, do you know anything of Townsend Spring's financial affairs just now?"

"Only what rumor brings me," replied the Englishman. "The market in Wall Street has been playing some very queer tricks of late, and Spring seems to be among the speculators who are liable any day to a very serious tumble. God help him and those three women, if he goes to smash this time! He's been put on his legs by friends so often before that there's nobody left, I'm afraid, if he should come to grief now.". . .

These words, spoken half at random, dwelt with Wainwright long after he had parted from Mr. Binghamton that night. They got into his pillow and murdered sleep. He had no memory for the eccentricities of Mrs. Bangs's guests; he failed to remember that the recent event at the club had made him food for antagonistic comments. He thought only of an unhappy girl, hesitating before an act of thrilling sacrifice. And mingled with the vision of her pale, troubled face, mingled with the warm sentiment of his own deep pity, something closely like self-contempt found a way to sting and chafe him, dealing hurts all the harsher because he again and again kept telling his own spirit that they were dealt against a resistant force of which honest self-respect formed the one vital origin.

XV.

HE went to the Springs' house early in the afternoon of the next day, asking simply for Ruth of the servant who admitted him. He had made a certain distinct resolve, which he was firmly bent upon carrying out. It was now very clear to him that he could never ask Ruth Cheever to become his wife. He felt that the struggle had begun and ended. It had been short, but hard. "I shall never marry any other woman," he told himself; "but I shall not marry her. It is decided."

In the conflict through which he had passed Wainwright had seemed to himself like a physician making a cool diagnosis of his own malady. He had put his hand, so to speak, on the throbbing arteries of his passion, and had calmly counted their strokes. In one sense he had been very deliberating, but the deliberation had been wrung from a pain whose uncontrolled impetus might have pushed him to the desperate surrender of all reflection. And the longer this introspective process lasted the more he had become convinced that his love fought against no merely selfish pride. If a worldly element entered into his reluctance, it was not one of captious fastidiousness. He had made imagination help reason in outlining the possibilities which would wait upon such a union. He had a very lofty view of marriage; for years he had clothed it, as regarded his own future, with a fine idealism. He felt that, however pure were Ruth herself, the surroundings from which he might take her would be those held by him as despicable; and he doubted his own power, in the years which would follow, always to forget from what soil he had plucked even so stainless a bloom. It would no longer be possible for him to live permanently away from his native country. He had learned to love that country, to identify it with the first earnest and wholesome interests of his life, and to desire to serve it hereafter as worthily as MIS best energies would permit If he married Ruth, no sea could roll between her and the kindred among whom he had found her. Their presence would remain, and he had finally assured himself that their presence must be a perpetual thorn in the flesh of all matrimonial harmony.

Thus Wainwright had decided, for thus it had been the effect of past environments upon a man of just his nature inevitably to decide. But the resolve which he had now made was full of a generously helpful longing; he wanted to place her beyond the necessity of marrying Mr. Amsterdam,—a contingency that dismayed him, as something hideous and sacrilegious.

Ruth was in the reception-room as he entered it. A gentleman was seated beside her, having his back turned to the door-way. Ruth could see Wainwright the moment that he appeared on the threshold, her face being in his direction. The fire on the hearth was wreathing itself about a solid plinth of coal. In the interspace between two rich-dyed Persian rugs, on the polished wooden floor, lay a square of winter sunshine. By an odd effect the light from a near window had flung the shadow on the gentleman who sat near Ruth, directly before her, in dark distinctness. The latter, following her look, turned, and revealed himself to be Mr. Abernethy. He rose and shook hands with Wainwright, who observed upon his swarthy face a discomposure unlike the furtive smile which usually seemed to sleep under its copious black moustache. Ruth appeared more worn than when he had left her last evening; her eyes had got dusky lines beneath them, and this made her continued pallor more evident; but she looked perfectly tranquil, and greeted the new-comer with gracious repose.

Wainwright had not been in the room five minutes, however, before he became conscious that the air was charged with some sort of hostility. Mr. Abernethy kept his black eyes fixed on the fire, occasionally thrusting a few words into the conversation between Ruth and Wainwright, as if spurred to do so by a sense of his own taciturnity. The result of this spasmodic process was most awkward and artificial.

"You've been creating quite a sensation at the Metropolitan," he suddenly said to Wainwright, breaking a little term of silence, during which the latter had indulged in a mute hope that he would go.

"I am sorry to hear it," replied Wainwright; 'I dislike sensations exceedingly, and to be he subject of one is very disagreeable."

"Upon my word," said Mr. Abernethy, with a laugh he had that always seemed further down in his throat than it ought to be, and like a sneer somehow put into sound, "I'm glad you snubbed that insupportable Gansevoort. He deserved snubbing. I've often thought I'd try it myself; but then those things are such bores."

"I did not find it a bore," said Wainwright. "I think, indeed, that I rather enjoyed it while it lasted. I confess to finding satisfaction in rapping people's toes when they over-step proper social boundaries."

He contrived to throw the least suspicion of sarcastic personality into his last words, and involuntarily, after speaking them, his eyes met Ruth's. Mr. Abernethy did not start, but he looked for an instant like a man who has restrained himself from starting.

"You'll become very unpopular," he said, "if you go in much for that style of reform." There seemed to be a vague hint of sullenness in his tones as he added, "Here in America I'm afraid we don't relish being told too plainly of our faults."

"That antipathy is common to all nations, and nearly all individuals," said Wainwright. His manner was entirely civil; he was still looking at Ruth. She had colored a little; he wondered why.

"I heard of the matter," she said, quietly. "But I have no doubt that report put words into your mouth, Mr. Wainwright, which you never spoke. The snow-ball must have grown very large, even in this short time."

"Please believe that I didn't set it rolling," said Wainwright, good-naturedly. I will tell you just what happened.". . . And he proceeded to relate the whole circumstance with a close adherence to facts. Mr. Abernethy sat staring at the fire while he spoke; occasionally he drummed with the fingers of one hand on the arm of his chair. He had extremely handsome hands; many ladies, in past times, had declared that they were one of his "fascinations;" the tapering olive fingers ended in pink, rounded nails, as glossy as burnished agate. Neither Wainwright nor Ruth took any note of his face; if they had done so they might have fancied that it resembled the face of a person who is slowly but steadily making up his mind.

As Wainwright finished Mr. Abernethy raised his eyes. He turned them upon Ruth. It is possible that the girl saw in them a cold, determined defiance.

"Pray, Miss Ruth," he said, very smoothly, yet with emphasis, "am I not to have the pleasure of seeing Miss Lyddy this morning?"

"Ruth bit her lip for a moment. But she returned the speaker's gaze with a peculiar, unflinching fixity. "No, Mr. Abernethy," she replied. "I think I told you, before Mr. Wainwright entered, that you could not see Lyddy."

"If I remember correctly, you said that she was at home?"

"Yes," replied Ruth, "she is at home."

There was a silence. Mr. Abernethy drew his chair closer toward the fire, and spread his hands out before its blaze, as if desirous of warming them. While still in a leaning posture, he again turned toward Ruth, saying,—

"It can't be possible that she or you may want to treat me rudely?"

Ruth rose. There was a flash in her eyes, and her lips were trembling; she looked indignant, and when she spoke there were vibrant traces of anger in her voice.

"I don't know what your purpose can be," she exclaimed, looking directly at the stooped figure before the fire-place, "unless it is to make me repeat the words I said a short while ago! They were very disagreeable words; I did not at all like to utter them, and I should not like to repeat them."

Mr. Abernethy slowly rose. Wainwright, who had also risen, out of deference to Ruth, was at no loss thoroughly to divine the situation. Mr. Abernethy showed a sort of sinister embarrassment; he had tried to employ a malicious stratagem, and had failed; he had found his match in Ruth, and the discovery demoralized him; every trace of his effrontery had fled. He was a person who had a rather well-won reputation for good manners, in the superficial significance of that term; a number of his feminine admirers were wont to say that he never "forgot himself."

He did not forget himself now. He seemed lo conquer his confusion while walking slowly across the room and pausing at the door-way. A smile had by this time lighted his dark features, leaving a little gleam of white teeth under his black moustache.

"I am very sorry," he said, quite softly, addressing Ruth, "that you should feel it necessary to break, in my case, the rules of hospitality; for you are a lady to whom I have always firmly believed that such rules must be sacred." He then addressed Wainwright, and without raising his voice managed to show an intonation of really piercing satire. "Most men," he continued, "are apt to neglect good-breeding when treated uncivilly, even if the offender be a woman; but I have been fortunate, per-haps, in having felt the near example of one who has gained so wide a reputation as a teacher of etiquette." He bowed, murmured "Good-morning," and disappeared into the outer hall. It was really a very effective departure; it could not have been better conducted by the most accomplished comedian of the genteel, modern, un-dramatic school. He had glided out of an almost pitiable strait with the dexterity of exceptional cleverness. The whole proceeding struck Wainwright as so ready and supple that he realized clearly, in that brief interval, what power of danger might consort with such skilled and parrying self-possession. Not a word was spoken between Wainwright and Ruth until they heard the hall-door outside sharply close, and were sure that Mr. Abernethy had gone. Then Wainwright exclaimed, louder than he perhaps knew, "I understand just what that man was aiming for! And you defeated him most valiantly. I congratulate you."

"He has not made me very angry," said Ruth, with a momentary choked sound in her voice. She sank into a chair, giving a slight laugh that was almost hysterical. "Perhaps he might have conquered me," she went on, "if you had not already heard just how affairs stood."

"I used my knowledge," replied Wainwright. "I put two and two together. You had been giving him his congé, in downright fashion, just before I arrived."

"Yes. I have so wanted to save poor foolish Lyddy, as you know. Yesterday I found that a new power had been put into my hands. Fanny, utterly alarmed and wretched, has begun to lean on me in the most supine way ever since" . . . She paused here, and again her color rose a little. "Well," she continued, with odd haste, "ever since I made her a certain promise. And so, invested with my new authority, I used it. I told her how the world must already be talking of Lyddy and that man's perilous addresses to the child. Fanny listened; she did not toss her head and call me a stupid prude; she actually made herself my ally, instead. We attacked Lyddy together. Fanny seconded all my grim admonitions. It was arranged that I should see Mr. Abernethy when he next called. That was to-day. I faced the enemy alone, as bravely as I could. He was very insolent and very gentlemanly, if you can understand how those two traits may be combined."

"I can—after what I have just seen."

"Well, I thought the battle was fought when you appeared. I fancy that he thought so, too. It had been made very clear to him that he must come here no more, and that Lyddy herself had so desired. But he sought to steal a march upon me, to spike my guns, using your unexpected presence as a means toward that end."

"He is a shocking fellow, and I want to hear no more about him," said Wainwright, after a silence had fallen between them. "I want to hear of something else," he added, measuredly.

"Of what else?" said Ruth, lifting her eyes to his face.

"Of your promise to your sister. Will you let me ask you what that was?"

Ruth started, changing color most noticeably. "I would rather not tell you," she said, in a low voice. "My telling you can do no good. It cannot alter matters."

"Do you mean," said Wainwright, with an imperative directness, "that you have promised Mrs. Spring to become the wife of Mr. Amsterdam?"

Ruth sat now with drooped eyes. "Yes, I do mean that," she at length murmured. She was making little creases with both hands in the front folds of her dress.

Wainwright felt a kind of inward tremor Several different responses rushed to his lips but he kept them all back, and quietly pondered, during the silence that ensued, what it would be best to say. What he presently did say was this:—

"Now I want you to make *me* a promise."

Before she could answer him he rose from the seat opposite her, which he had lately taken, and went up to where she sat, with his right hand outstretched.

"I want you to promise me that you will not accept Mr. Amsterdam for three days."

As she again looked up at him he felt the stab of a misgiving lest she had already written or spoken to her suitor, and the bond he required was therefore impossible. But her answer dissipated this gloomy doubt.

"I see no reason," she said, "why I should make this promise to you, Mr. Wainwright."

"But I do. I see a most excellent reason. Won't you take my hand and promise? A little delay can do no harm."

She saw entreaty on his face; she heard it in his tones. She gave him her hand, rising. "Very well," she said. But suddenly she withdrew her hand, though he retained it almost with force. "Oh, why," she exclaimed, plaintively, while a bitter distress clouded her face,—"why need I postpone this wretched compact? It must be made now, and it had best be made while I have steeled my nerves, rallied my courage. I don't know what may happen to me in those three days. I am sorry that I made you this promise. Let me take it back."

Ruth spoke with random heat. Her look was full of misery; it wrung Wainwright to the heart. She had receded many paces away from him, but he again hurried to her side.

"You are right," he cried, "when you say that you don't know what may happen in those three days! You don't know what help may come to you. I am going to try and help you. I shall try my best."

"You?" she faltered.

"Yes." He caught her hand once more. He pressed it hard, but the pressure lasted only an instant. Then he walked rapidly to the door, and as he turned, on reaching its threshold, he saw her standing by the fireplace, staring after him with a bewildered gaze.

He would have told her more, but he felt that he was himself only too ignorant of what it might be possible for him to do. And he dared not kindle in her breast any full name of hope. As yet he had the right only to set a feeble spark there.

XVI.

IN the former days of Wall Street, nearly a score of years ago, when war held the fate of our nation in its bloody balance, and the price of gold vibrated with heavy changes almost hourly, the fever of speculation passed all limits. Then it was not a rare thing for brokers to earn from eight hundred to ten thousand dollars a day in commissions. More than a hundred millions were realized in sales. New York never wore so opulent and festal an aspect. Luxurious carriages rolled through the Park; Delmonico's best resources were taxed in the giving of artistic dinners; the city showed a ceaseless variety of balls and receptions. The mania of speculation raged in all departments of life. Brokers offices were crowded with customers; the clerk invested his precious salary; the old man staked his slender annuity; the widow risked her all. Then darker times followed: heavy defalcations convulsed the Street; periods of comparative quiet were succeeded by stormy episodes. Government, through the sudden sales of millions, wrought havoc and dismay. The prices of bullion strangely vacillated; loans would abruptly go up and stocks would fall with a crash. Then came three years of dull monotony in the market, and at last the disastrous horrors of Black Friday. For some time previous to this woful event, an approaching tempest had been observable, and there had been evidences of a formidable clique movement. The clearances of the Gold Exchange Bank had markedly increased. A large number of operators attempted to pull down gold, but its price rose with startling speed. The indomitable "men of Erie," with the fearless, insolent, and astute James Fisk at their head, were hotly at work. In one morning gold shot from 145 to 162½. Fisk's life was threatened. Men saw their last dollars disappearing in the turbid whirlpool of that frightful complication. New York Central, Hudson, Pittsburg, and Northwest shares fell at a ruinous rate. The dread of yet higher prices in gold produced a universal agony. Faces pale with despair gleamed from windows and along pavements; one young broker, whose losses had been enormous, was carried home almost lifeless from the bursting of an artery. In this hour, too, when everybody's credit was suspected by his neighbor, old animosities leapt up and dealt hidden blows. It was a time of anarchy, chaos, unexampled suspense. The stanchest men now recall Black Friday with a shudder, and many will have the most solemn reasons for remembering it to the close of their lives.

These calamitous days are now past; peace has brought its quieter victories; but Wall Street still remains a prodigious fact. It speaks volumes to the thoughtful looker-on. It is our social boiling-point, at which those fierce forces, wrestling beneath our surface, find a continuous wrathful vent. Being the direct result of our imprudent modes of living, our tendency to pluck the fruits of all circumstance before they have come to ripeness, it now offers a constant intoxicating temptation to many of our best minds, as these enter, year after year, upon the fight of life, vitiating and perverting that which a healthful serenity of occupation might have developed into valuable and brilliant maturity. As in all similar cases, the love for this sort of gaming grows with what it feeds upon. Ordinary commercial dealings would be tame indeed to those who have tasted these thrilling excitements. Even the jeopardies of a military career could not prove their fitting substitute, with its intervals of tedium, its dreary fatigues, and its necessity for mechanical discipline. Nevertheless, if speculation be a disease, the disease is one worthy of close attention. Its workings certainly possess a morbid harmony by no means beneath the study of the analyst. The fatal effects of this overstrained life can be told by the dark experiences of many a physician. Slow and noiseless are the casualties resulting from it; but victims are forever falling in this fight of tense-strung nerves and rivalry-spurred brains. A mere walk through the streets thus devoted to the ceaseless struggles of gamester against gamester will impress one, whose scrutiny is on the alert, with a sense of some new malarial atmosphere. Those whom we meet often have a restless, disquieted step. If one of them be an acquaintance, and we pause to greet mm, the chances are that he will salute us with an absent, flurried demeanor. We are not of his hazardous and combative world; we belong among the more tranquil dwellers of earth; we have not been inoculated with his own goading distemper; we are mere lookers-on in Vienna, and Vienna has something better to do than concern itself with our humdrum neutrality.

Wainwright was filled with impressions more or less of tins sort as he passed through a certain portion of Wall Street on the day that followed his last interview with Ruth. He had made an effort, during the previous afternoon and evening, to see Townsend Spring; but two separate searches for this gentleman at the Metropolitan Club had proved equally futile. He had learned Spring's business address late the night before, and was now making practical use of this knowledge. It was a little after eleven o'clock when he entered a small office, where two clerks sat at two desks, and a shabby, grisly man, in an overcoat that wanted several important buttons, stood cleaning his nails with a dingy penknife. One of the clerks, a thin, pale stripling, with an ink-spot on his cheek that made him look thinner and paler, answered Wainwright's inquiry for Mr. Spring, stating that the latter was at present in the Board. Wainwright politely asked where the "Board" could be found, and was immediately favored with a hard stare from the other clerk, who wore a dapper cravat in the shape of a large butterfly, and had a head of short, close curls parted accurately in the middle. Then the two clerks momentarily gazed at each other, as though this distressing betrayal of ignorance was something very unusual in the experience of both. Presently the stripling with the ink-spot gave Wainwright the necessary instructions, and he departed in search of the Stock Exchange.

Not very long after this, he stood at a doorway opening directly off a narrow street, and requested a porter on guard at its entrance to bring him where he could speak with Mr. Spring. But before the words had passed his lips he became aware that a wild tumult was taking place in an immense chamber beyond. Hundreds of voices seemed shrieking in furious concert, and he had a vision of numberless male figures pressed together like an insurgent mob, and lifting their arms in savage gesticulation. The porter, a stolid and impassive personage, shook his head, and declared to Wainwright in brief, civil terms that he must "go up-stairs." Wainwright went up-stairs, wondering. He soon found himself in a gallery overlooking the mad turmoil of forms and voices. Now and then one shrill, querulous cry would rise above the prevailing bedlam, only to be drowned, a second later, by that of some more stentorian shouter. The uproar and the insane gestures accompanying it were partly directed toward a sort of presidential rostrum, where sat a gentleman, who gazed down upon all this turbulence with the unmoved calm of a sphinx, now and then making raps with a gavel. By degrees Wainwright grew accustomed to the noisy throng; he separated one individuality from another; here and there he recognized the face of an acquaintance. But there were many whom he did not recognize, and among the excited bidders he began to observe all varieties of visage, the indices of countless differing temperaments. Yonder was the fresh-cheeked, beard less youth, whom fate had snatched from the competitions of the college curriculum to waste his adolescence in these far more unwholesome contests, and make him old and jaded long before his time. Here was the shrewd-eyed, sallow operator, veteran of unnumbered financial frays, weary to the bone of this end less contention, yet remaining in it with something of that doleful pertinacity which makes the victim of opium still cleave to his pernicious drug. Here was the stout, oleaginous vulgarian, bejeweled, glaringly dapper, voluminous moustache, and trousers an extravagant plaid. Here was the decorous club-man, genteel to his finger-tips, a marvel of good style. Here rose some grimy, red-lipped Abraham Isaacs, in whom the usual prudence of his race had been conquered, perhaps, by a longing rapidly to amass thousands. And nearly all were yelling with an awful, strident volubility. Many, too, were using gestures that would not have looked amiss among the tumble habitants of a far-away cocoa grove.

Naturally, Wainwright sought for Townsend Spring's face amid the multitude. For some time he was unsuccessful in discovering the man whom he had come hither to meet. But at length, happening to cast his eyes into a certain corner of the huge apartment, where several men were standing in apparently brisk converse that bore no seeming relation to the clamors going on so near them, he perceived the object of his search. Spring had thrust both hands into his pockets, and wore a smile of broad good-humor. He was speaking, as it looked, with jovial vehemence. Now and then he burst into a laugh, and bent his body for ward, as he did so, with lively mirth. Wainwright was astonished at these evidences of light-heartedness, but found a ready explanation of them in the reckless, blunted nature of the man, for whom impending or even existent ruin was doubtless a stroke to be met with blurt bravado. He despaired of attracting Spring's notice, from that elevated position; but suddenly the latter chanced to raise his eyes, discerned Wainwright, and gave him a recognizing nod. Immediately Wainwright made a signal, which Spring showed prompt signs that he understood. He shouted forth, "All right, old fellow! I'll come up." And very soon afterward he came up.

"So you're down here to take a look at the Board!" he exclaimed, vigorously grasping Wainwright's hand. "Crazy old hole, isn't it? Suppose it scared you at first."

"Well, it was rather frightful."

Spring put both arms on the balustrade of the gallery, and stared downward for a moment. Then he turned to his companion with jerky suddenness, pounding with one hand heavily on the wooden railing.

"By heavens, sir," he cried, "I'm the happiest boy in it to-day! I'm deuced if the luck hasn't gone dead with me this morning. It's made Towney Spring a man again. The market's changed, and I've done one of the neatest operations this street has seen in ten days. Some time ago, don't you see, I caught a rumor that a pool was being made on North West Common. I kept a sharp lookout; soon I got so sure of the thing I'd have bet my last dollar on it. I bought sixty day calls on five thousand share of that stock, I was so certain it was bound to move. Meanwhile, it kept me poor for a devil of a time. Every dollar I got I put right into it. Yesterday the stock did begin to move. This morning it boomed and now I'm in clover. I've just sent a telegram up home to Fanny. She'll be devilish glad. Poor little woman, I left her half frightened out of her wits. Things looked so infernally black for about a week past that I thought it was all up with yours truly, d—d——if I didn't! But now there'll be plain sailing for a good while,—no more beating against the wind. I'll pay up every dollar I owe, and start fair again, with a good stiff surplus,—hanged if I don't!"

"I congratulate you most heartily," said Wainwright. He felt a great inward thankfulness. He almost liked Townsend Spring at that moment. In imagination he could see Ruth's face brightening with infinite relief.

Spring clapped him sharply on the shoulder. "Can I do anything for you, old boy?" he said, cheerily abrupt. "I've got a heap of things to 'tend to, but I'd have come up here even if you hadn't beckoned. The fact is, Wainwright, my man, I want to thank you for that little service you did Fanny. It was perfectly beastly in her to ask you; it made me madder than blazes when I heard it. I gave her the tallest kind of a lecture, you can bet. But it was devilish kind of you to go and see that confounded dressmaker, and then do what you did."

"Pray, think no more about it," said Wainwright.

A little later he separated from Spring, and went up town. His joy at Ruth's deliverance began to take tinges of melancholy during the journey. He had sought Townsend Spring with the ardent wish to aid and save her; he had had no other motive, and that had already grown a burning desire. He now felt that all bond between himself and Ruth was suddenly shattered. It was like the solid ground failing to bear his feet. What further right had he to approach her now? His past resolve rose before him in stern requisition; it imperiously demanded fulfillment. "And yet I will see her," he mused. "I must see her once again,—if it be for the last time in both our lives!"

XVII.

HE had to wait a brief while for Ruth before she joined him in the small reception-room. The whole chamber breathed of memories, now. On this chair she had sat; on yonder lounge she had thrown herself, when the misery of her coming fate had sent that unwonted surge through mind and frame, leveling her like a broken reed. At yonder fire-place she had stood, pale, slender, lovely, shadowed to his thought by the menace of a bitter doom. Near yonder table he had felt the parting clasp of her cool, smooth hand, The whole room spoke to him, and in a silent dialect of regret!

She came in, presently. He was surprised to see none of the enlivenment he had prophesied in her serious, patient mien.

"I have heard the good news, he said, after they were both seated. "I need not tell you what great pleasure it has given me."

"You mean. . . about Townsend?" she replied, hesitating.

"Yes. I was in Wall Street not long ago. He told me of the telegram he had sent Mrs. Spring."

Ruth slowly nodded. "It has quite exhilarated Fanny. She is a new person. She has gone out,—I think to buy something. She generally buys something, in these cases. It is her way of showing her thanks to fate."

"And what will be **your** way? "

"Mine?"

"Yes,—at your escape."

"I do not understand." She had lifted her brow in surprise.

"Ah," exclaimed Wainwright, "you can't mean that **you** have nothing to be grateful for!"

She looked at him intently. "I have nothing" she answered.

"But you are free. You are released from that hateful compact with your sister." "Oh, no," she said.

"For Heaven's sake." cried Wainwright 'what do you mean?"

His excitement seemed to make her calmer. "Townsend has gambled and won. How long will it be before he may gamble and lose? You don't know him,—you don't know Fanny. To-day's temporary turn of luck will only give her a keener sense of to-morrow's possible mishaps. She will hold me unrelentingly to my promise. The danger that has threatened her will only make her more distrustful of the future."

Wainwright's face was very dark as he said, quickly and harshly, "Demand your money from Townsend Spring now. Go from this house. Go to your former friends in Massachusetts."

Ruth shook her head; a pained smile was on her lips. "I think I once told you," she said "that in spite of all Fanny's faults I love her. She does not care for me, but I care for her. I can't help it. It sometimes seems wrong for me to feel toward her as I do. I know just how cold she is,—just how selfish. But when I picture the misery that may come to her, I". . . She paused, and her voice broke.

"You are willing to ruin your own life!" exclaimed Wainwright, finishing her sentence with a ring of intolerance and ire. He almost sprang to his feet as he spoke. Just then a laugh sounded near the closed door. In another instant the door was opened, and Mrs. Spring entered, followed by Mr. Amsterdam.

Wainwright never afterward remembered the greetings that followed. For a little while he felt incapable of speaking, of even listening. He saw Mrs. Spring untie her bonnet-strings, and move here and there about the room at an airy and dainty pace. He knew that she was rattling on with her most loquacious freedom, but the sense of her words quite evaded him.

"Mr. Amsterdam and I met in the Avenue," she was saying, "and we had a long walk together. He thinks I looked charming at the Bodensteins' ball. I was under the same impression myself, but it's always delightful to have one's secret convictions of that sort confirmed by good authority. Ruth, he actually remembers all the details of my trimmings; isn't it sweet of him? I'll venture to say it is more than Mr. Wainwright does." She tossed her bonnet on the table, and sank into a chair; she was giving her hair little light touches, to see that it was properly ordered. "Why don't you both sit down?" she exclaimed, looking at Wainwright and Mr. Amsterdam with two rapid turns of the head.

The latter at once seated himself near Ruth, but Wainwright remained standing, with one hand on the mantel. He had not caught the meaning of her words; his mind was otherwise employed.

Mrs. Spring began to unbutton her gloves and draw them off with leisurely slowness. "Ruth, dear," she said, looking straight at her sister, "we have been talking a great deal about you. Mr. Amsterdam has got such an absurd idea! He fancies that you don't like him. I told him how mistaken he was. I told him just to ask you, and find out the real facts. And he means to do it" Here Mrs. Spring burst into one of her gayest laughs. She threw back her head; her eyes were twinkling with a mischievous glee. She was in one of her sauciest humors, and behind it seemed to sparkle a steely malice. Life had turned rose-color with her; Townsend was "on his feet" again. The old mood of tormenting Ruth had come back with her sudden blissful sense of prosperity. She had secure faith in her sister's promise; there could be no harm in trying her beloved trick of embarrassing people by bold thrusts at sensitive places. She inwardly thought the man whom Ruth was to marry a gloomy, methodical bore of a person. She had always poked fun at him in her daring, jaunty way. What harm to indulge this sport now, when she need only raise a finger and seal the precious engagement? "Don't deny that you mean to make an inquiry into the real state of Ruth's feelings," she galloped on, with another ripple of laughter, addressing Mr. Amsterdam. "Mr. Wainwright and I will give you a lesson, if you're bashful. We're both practiced teachers. We'll teach Ruth, too."

Wainwright was listening now. He had grown pale.

Ruth, however, had flushed deeply. She rose to her feet. "Fanny," she exclaimed, "you are cruel!"

"Oh, pshaw!" retorted Mrs. Spring, shrugging her shoulders, but perhaps feeling that her reckless tongue had tripped too rashly. 'You know I was only in fun. You never could take a joke."

"Some of your jokes are not easy to take," said Wainwright, measuring each word. He held one hand clenched behind him, concealed from sight.

Ruth turned and looked at him, briefly but meaningly. He read an actual desperation in her look. It seemed to say to him, "I have borne enough; I will bear no more."

She again addressed Mrs. Spring. Her voice was full of agitated throbs; her bosom showed how quick her breath was coming.

"Fanny." she said, "I will not endure this mockery any further. You know what I mean. I refuse to be held, as you have held me so long, the target of your impudent jests."

Mrs. Spring was genuinely frightened. She laughed again, but the laugh rang false "Oh, good heavens!" she said. "I hope you are not going to make a scene for nothing!"

At this moment Mr. Amsterdam got up from his chair. As he did so, the fact of his extreme height produced a sort of visual shock. He approached Ruth, speaking in his precise, formal way.

"Miss Ruth," he said, "I think your sister meant no harm."

Ruth gave a scornful laugh. She had controlled her anger for so many months that now it seemed to have whirled away all prudence. Recent events had severely unnerved her; for days past her life had been one incessant crushing down of natural emotions. Her final vow of sacrifice had taxed heroism with wrenching force. She had felt as though she were writing the vow out in her blood. Yesterday she had seen her sister abject, supplicating, blinded with hysterical tears. She had pitied her, and yielded to her inhuman demand. Then, in a few hours, the old insolent demeanor had returned. . . . But there was still another reason for the girl's anger. That reason—perhaps most cogent of all—was the presence of Wainwright.

She did not give Mr. Amsterdam a glance after he had spoken. She kept her eyes fixed on Mrs. Spring. "I will not do what I told you I would do," she said, with husky speed. "I don't know what you have told Mr. Amsterdam." She made an impetuous gesture with one hand toward that gentleman, who still stood at tier side, lank, decorous, distressed, with his peculiar upper lip set in stony repose, like an unintentionally comic emblem of silence. "Hereafter," Ruth hurried on, "I shall fix my conduct by wiser rules than any your heartless will may dictate. Oh, be sure of this, Fanny! I need say no more,—you understand me." She now took several hasty steps toward the door-way.

"Stop!" said Mrs. Spring, turning pale as she also rose. "I will go with you, Ruth. I do **not** understand you. I wish to speak with you for a moment. I wish to ask you"—

"I know what you wish to ask me!" cried Ruth. "And I answer you 'no!' . . . No! she repeated, with a flash in her eyes as they met her sister's. "Is that enough? I break my promise. I don't care,—I break it." She passed from the room.

Wainwright instantly followed her. He overtook her just as she had placed her foot on the first step of the staircase. She looked round and saw him. Then he caught her hand, and held it hard,—so hard that she could not free it if she would.

"Will you be my wife? he said, very low, yet quite distinctly.

Ruth burst into tears. "Ah," she murmured, "you are asking me because you pity me!"

"I am asking you because I love you," he said.

Her cheeks had fired to scarlet. His clasp upon her hand was slackening a little, and she drew it away. Without another word she turned and went up-stairs. Wainwright still followed her. Knowing that he did so, she paused in the small central hall, near one of the drawing-rooms, rich and dim with the winter-afternoon light.

"Let me speak with you a moment here," said Wainwright, pointing toward this room. His voice was deeply tender as he faced her.

"Not now, not now," she said. She had already placed her hand on the banister of the next staircase. Again he put his own hand about hers, but this time with a soft touch. She did not resist him; she stood there trembling, with the tears falling swift and large from her uplifted eyes.

"Yes," he said, "let it be now. I want you to sit down at my side and listen to me for a little while. It need only be for a little while, if you so wish. But let it be now."

She yielded, and he led her into the quiet, vacant room. They sat down together on one of the sofas. . . .

Nearly an hour afterward Mrs. Spring came up-stairs, and found them thus seated. The room had grown somewhat dimmer.

Wainwright rose as soon as the lady had crossed the threshold.

Mrs. Spring," he said, "I have as e your sister to be my wife, and she has consented."

Mrs. Spring remained perfectly silent for at least two minutes; and two minutes of silence, under circumstances like the present, form an appreciable interval.

"I am very much surprised," she presently said, in a voice so constrained and grave that it did not seem her own. "But I congratulate you both." She went up to Wainwright, all its wonted briskness absent from her step, and shook hands with him. Some adornment on her person gave a tinkle amid the extreme stillness as she did so; but it was only a faint tinkle; its effect had an uncharacteristic tame-ness.

Afterward she walked toward Ruth, and stood before her. "Ruth," she said, "I wish you the greatest happiness. Won't you kiss me?"

Ruth rose and kissed her.

"I suppose I'm frightfully *de trop,*" then said, with a thin, nervous laugh, moving toward the wide door-way. "I thought something important must be happening up here; but I didn't suspect anything quite so important as this."

"What does it mean?" questioned Wainwright of Ruth, as they heard her descending the stairs. "Is she glad?"

"I think she is glad," Ruth answered. There was a slight pause, then. "She always liked you. I don't undertake to say why, but you always represented one of her preferences." . . .

Meanwhile Mrs. Spring went down into the reception-room, where Mr. Amsterdam awaited her. She remained for some time in close conversation with this gentleman. At the conclusion of their interview Mr. Amsterdam rose, bade her a courteous, exact good-by, and left the house. He left it for the last time in his life, and he went away to suffer. He was forty-nine years old; he was a widower with six children; but he went away to suffer.

Wainwright smiled to himself while he sat alone in the chamber of his hotel, rather late that same evening. The scruples, prejudices, theories, which had dealt him such distress but a few hours ago had vanished into air; they had left not a wrack behind them. Beside the precious discovery of possessing Ruth's love, and the sweet recognition of what a vital warmth fed his own, all harsh distrust of their future wedded contentment had grown serene certainty. A great and holy truth had become manifest to him, and he looked with cloudless vision straight at its brightness. It had not solved the meaning of life, since that grace is not given the best of us; but it had taught him why so many are content to live on with that meaning unsolved, and stifle complaint till the last wound has made the last scar. He had cared for no woman before as he now cared for Ruth; and that first and finest of human sentiments, whose sanctity had thus far addressed him only through imagination, at last had blent itself with actual events, and run a shining thread across the duller fabric of experience. It was like the difference between seeing the bird go white and fleet along its native blue, and having it perch sleek and fearless on his wrist, to feed from his hand. The dawn had dispelled all his phantoms; he found it very easy to gaze stoically upon the coming kinship with Mrs. Spring, and even her husband as well. He wondered whether, in any case, he would have held to those frigid lines of reasoning whose calculation now looked to him so finically geometric. He even asked himself whether the struggle through which he had lately passed was not a mock battle, after all,—a sort of light-infantry exercise, from which the passions stood aloof with their big guns, while a clatter of blank cartridges raged harmlessly. Had logic ever learned enough engineering to set lasting masonries against the current of such a love as his for Ruth? Or could that current, deep and strong as he now knew it, ever have enslaved itself by turning the monotonous mill of dreary theoretic self-denial? Judging after the event, Wainwright imperatively declared that any but his recent course would have been impossible. He may or he may not have judged rightly. Circumstance will sometimes lead us to happiness by so unexpected a bend in the pathway that we forget how much we owe the guide, and boast that our own feet have secured us the fortunate goal. . . .

During the next day the news of Wainwright's engagement traveled rapidly among certain social cliques, and it is credible that Mrs. Spring may have had a hand in this expeditious transit. Early in the evening of the same day he was on the point of quitting his apartment, when Mr. Binghamton suddenly announced himself, quite bristling with congratulations.

"My dear Wainwright," he exclaimed, "I am delighted! I can't help but feel like an accomplice in your good luck,—and it is an enormous piece of good luck for you, as I haven't the least hesitation in affirming. You remember what agreeable things I said of that charming girl just before I made you acquainted with her? Let me hug the delusion that my halcyon recommendations have had something to do with this blissful result!"

"I haven't the least objection," replied Wainwright, with a smile, "to your believing that you brought about the match."

"Thanks," said Mr. Binghamton, with a second effusive shake of his friend's hand. "Now you are an American indeed!"

"Yes, I am certainly an American."

"But you must naturalize yourself, as they call it, in other ways. You must, truly! I feel that I haven't done with you yet, by any means. You have shown me qualities that positively tempt further development. I mean, of course, in a purely national way. . . . You don't intend taking your bride to England, by the bye?"

"Never permanently," answered Wainwright, amused, but with decision. "We shall live here."

"I am glad to hear it. I thought as much. And now that you have acknowledged your country, I want you . . . yes, by Jove, I want you to adorn it."

"Ah," I wish that I could!"

"Nonsense! You can! There is always something to be done for a land in which those best suited to serve it serve it so ill." Here Mr. Binghamton seized Wainwright's hand for the third time. "Egad, old fellow," he cried, "you shall run for Congress!"

Wainwright was silent a moment. "I should like very much to run for Congress," he presently said.

www.bookjungle.com *email: sales@bookjungle.com fax: 630-214-0564 mail: Book Jungle PO Box 2226 Champaign, IL 61825*

The Codes Of Hammurabi And Moses
W. W. Davies

QTY

The discovery of the Hammurabi Code is one of the greatest achievements of archaeology, and is of paramount interest, not only to the student of the Bible, but also to all those interested in ancient history...

Religion **ISBN:** *1-59462-338-4* **Pages:132**

MSRP $12.95

The Theory of Moral Sentiments
Adam Smith

QTY

This work from 1749. contains original theories of conscience amd moral judgment and it is the foundation for systemof morals.

Philosophy **ISBN:** *1-59462-777-0* **Pages:536**

MSRP $19.95

Jessica's First Prayer
Hesba Stretton

QTY

In a screened and secluded corner of one of the many railway-bridges which span the streets of London there could be seen a few years ago, from five o'clock every morning until half past eight, a tidily set-out coffee-stall, consisting of a trestle and board, upon which stood two large tin cans, with a small fire of charcoal burning under each so as to keep the coffee boiling during the early hours of the morning when the work-people were thronging into the city on their way to their daily toil...

Pages:84

Childrens **ISBN:** *1-59462-373-2* *MSRP $9.95*

My Life and Work
Henry Ford

QTY

Henry Ford revolutionized the world with his implementation of mass production for the Model T automobile. Gain valuable business insight into his life and work with his own auto-biography... "We have only started on our development of our country we have not as yet, with all our talk of wonderful progress, done more than scratch the surface. The progress has been wonderful enough but..."

Pages:300

Biographies/ **ISBN:** *1-59462-198-5* *MSRP $21.95*

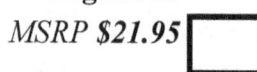

The Art of Cross-Examination
Francis Wellman

QTY

I presume it is the experience of every author, after his first book is published upon an important subject, to be almost overwhelmed with a wealth of ideas and illustrations which could readily have been included in his book, and which to his own mind, at least, seem to make a second edition inevitable. Such certainly was the case with me; and when the first edition had reached its sixth impression in five months, I rejoiced to learn that it seemed to my publishers that the book had met with a sufficiently favorable reception to justify a second and considerably enlarged edition. ..

Reference   ISBN: *1-59462-647-2*

Pages:412

MSRP $19.95

On the Duty of Civil Disobedience
Henry David Thoreau

QTY

Thoreau wrote his famous essay, On the Duty of Civil Disobedience, as a protest against an unjust but popular war and the immoral but popular institution of slave-owning. He did more than write—he declined to pay his taxes, and was hauled off to gaol in consequence. Who can say how much this refusal of his hastened the end of the war and of slavery ?

Law   ISBN: *1-59462-747-9*

Pages:48

MSRP $7.45

Dream Psychology Psychoanalysis for Beginners
Sigmund Freud

QTY

Sigmund Freud, born Sigismund Schlomo Freud (May 6, 1856 - September 23, 1939), was a Jewish-Austrian neurologist and psychiatrist who co-founded the psychoanalytic school of psychology. Freud is best known for his theories of the unconscious mind, especially involving the mechanism of repression; his redefinition of sexual desire as mobile and directed towards a wide variety of objects; and his therapeutic techniques, especially his understanding of transference in the therapeutic relationship and the presumed value of dreams as sources of insight into unconscious desires.

Dream Psychology
Psychoanalysis for Beginners

Sigmund Freud

Psychology   ISBN: *1-59462-905-6*

Pages:196

MSRP $15.45

The Miracle of Right Thought
Orison Swett Marden

QTY

Believe with all of your heart that you will do what you were made to do. When the mind has once formed the habit of holding cheerful, happy, prosperous pictures, it will not be easy to form the opposite habit. It does not matter how improbable or how far away this realization may see, or how dark the prospects may be, if we visualize them as best we can, as vividly as possible, hold tenaciously to them and vigorously struggle to attain them, they will gradually become actualized, realized in the life. But a desire, a longing without endeavor, a yearning abandoned or held indifferently will vanish without realization.

Pages:360

Self Help   ISBN: *1-59462-644-8*

MSRP $25.45

QTY

The Rosicrucian Cosmo-Conception Mystic Christianity *by Max Heindel*   ISBN: 1-59462-188-8   **$38.95**
The Rosicrucian Cosmo-conception is not dogmatic, neither does it appeal to any other authority than the reason of the student. It is: not controversial, but is: sent forth in the, hope that it may help to clear...
New Age/Religion Pages 646

Abandonment To Divine Providence *by Jean-Pierre de Caussade*   ISBN: 1-59462-228-0   **$25.95**
"The Rev. Jean Pierre de Caussade was one of the most remarkable spiritual writers of the Society of Jesus in France in the 18th Century. His death took place at Toulouse in 1751. His works have gone through many editions and have been republished...
Inspirational/Religion Pages 400

Mental Chemistry *by Charles Haanel*   ISBN: 1-59462-192-6   **$23.95**
Mental Chemistry allows the change of material conditions by combining and appropriately utilizing the power of the mind. Much like applied chemistry creates something new and unique out of careful combinations of chemicals the mastery of mental chemistry...
New Age Pages 354

The Letters of Robert Browning and Elizabeth Barret Barrett 1845-1846 vol II   ISBN: 1-59462-193-4   **$35.95**
by Robert Browning and Elizabeth Barrett
Biographies Pages 596

Gleanings In Genesis (volume I) *by Arthur W. Pink*   ISBN: 1-59462-130-6   **$27.45**
Appropriately has Genesis been termed "the seed plot of the Bible" for in it we have, in germ form, almost all of the great doctrines which are afterwards fully developed in the books of Scripture which follow...
Religion/Inspirational Pages 420

The Master Key *by L. W. de Laurence*   ISBN: 1-59462-001-6   **$30.95**
In no branch of human knowledge has there been a more lively increase of the spirit of research during the past few years than in the study of Psychology, Concentration and Mental Discipline. The requests for authentic lessons in Thought Control, Mental Discipline and...   *New Age/Business Pages 422*

The Lesser Key Of Solomon Goetia *by L. W. de Laurence*   ISBN: 1-59462-092-X   **$9.95**
This translation of the first book of the "Lernegton" which is now for the first time made accessible to students of Talismanic Magic was done, after careful collation and edition, from numerous Ancient Manuscripts in Hebrew, Latin, and French...
New Age/Occult Pages 92

Rubaiyat Of Omar Khayyam *by Edward Fitzgerald*   ISBN:1-59462-332-5   **$13.95**
Edward Fitzgerald, whom the world has already learned, in spite of his own efforts to remain within the shadow of anonymity, to look upon as one of the rarest poets of the century, was born at Bredfield, in Suffolk, on the 31st of March, 1809. He was the third son of John Purcell...   *Music Pages 172*

Ancient Law *by Henry Maine*   ISBN: 1-59462-128-4   **$29.95**
The chief object of the following pages is to indicate some of the earliest ideas of mankind, as they are reflected in Ancient Law, and to point out the relation of those ideas to modern thought.
Religiom/History Pages 452

Far-Away Stories *by William J. Locke*   ISBN: 1-59462-129-2   **$19.45**
"Good wine needs no bush, but a collection of mixed vintages does. And this book is just such a collection. Some of the stories I do not want to remain buried for ever in the museum files of dead magazine-numbers an author's not unpardonable vanity..."
Fiction Pages 272

Life of David Crockett *by David Crockett*   ISBN: 1-59462-250-7   **$27.45**
"Colonel David Crockett was one of the most remarkable men of the times in which he lived. Born in humble life, but gifted with a strong will, an indomitable courage, and unremitting perseverance...
Biographies/New Age Pages 424

Lip-Reading *by Edward Nitchie*   ISBN: 1-59462-206-X   **$25.95**
Edward B. Nitchie, founder of the New York School for the Hard of Hearing, now the Nitchie School of Lip-Reading, Inc, wrote "LIP-READING Principles and Practice". The development and perfecting of this meritorious work on lip-reading was an undertaking...   *How-to Pages 400*

A Handbook of Suggestive Therapeutics, Applied Hypnotism, Psychic Science   ISBN: 1-59462-214-0   **$24.95**
by Henry Munro
Health/New Age/Health/Self-help Pages 376

A Doll's House: and Two Other Plays *by Henrik Ibsen*   ISBN: 1-59462-112-8   **$19.95**
Henrik Ibsen created this classic when in revolutionary 1848 Rome. Introducing some striking concepts in playwriting for the realist genre, this play has been studied the world over.
Fiction/Classics/Plays 308

The Light of Asia *by sir Edwin Arnold*   ISBN: 1-59462-204-3   **$13.95**
In this poetic masterpiece, Edwin Arnold describes the life and teachings of Buddha. The man who was to become known as Buddha to the world was born as Prince Gautama of India but he rejected the worldly riches and abandoned the reigns of power when...   *Religion/History/Biographies Pages 170*

The Complete Works of Guy de Maupassant *by Guy de Maupassant*   ISBN: 1-59462-157-8   **$16.95**
"For days and days, nights and nights, I had dreamed of that first kiss which was to consecrate our engagement, and I knew not on what spot I should put my lips..."
Fiction/Classics Pages 240

The Art of Cross-Examination *by Francis L. Wellman*   ISBN: 1-59462-309-0   **$26.95**
Written by a renowned trial lawyer, Wellman imparts his experience and uses case studies to explain how to use psychology to extract desired information through questioning.
How-to/Science/Reference Pages 408

Answered or Unanswered? *by Louisa Vaughan*   ISBN: 1-59462-248-5   **$10.95**
Miracles of Faith in China
Religion Pages 112

The Edinburgh Lectures on Mental Science (1909) *by Thomas*   ISBN: 1-59462-008-3   **$11.95**
This book contains the substance of a course of lectures recently given by the writer in the Queen Street Hail, Edinburgh. Its purpose is to indicate the Natural Principles governing the relation between Mental Action and Material Conditions...
New Age/Psychology Pages 148

Ayesha *by H. Rider Haggard*   ISBN: 1-59462-301-5   **$24.95**
Verily and indeed it is the unexpected that happens! Probably if there was one person upon the earth from whom the Editor of this, and of a certain previous history, did not expect to hear again...
Classics Pages 380

Ayala's Angel *by Anthony Trollope*   ISBN: 1-59462-352-X   **$29.95**
The two girls were both pretty, but Lucy who was twenty-one who supposed to be simple and comparatively unattractive, whereas Ayala was credited, as her Bombwhat romantic name might show, with poetic charm and a taste for romance. Ayala when her father died was nineteen...   *Fiction Pages 484*

The American Commonwealth *by James Bryce*   ISBN: 1-59462-286-8   **$34.45**
An interpretation of American democratic political theory. It examines political mechanics and society from the perspective of Scotsman James Bryce
Politics Pages 572

Stories of the Pilgrims *by Margaret P. Pumphrey*   ISBN: 1-59462-116-0   **$17.95**
This book explores pilgrims religious oppression in England as well as their escape to Holland and eventual crossing to America on the Mayflower, and their early days in New England...
History Pages 268

QTY

The Fasting Cure *by Sinclair Upton*   ISBN: *1-59462-222-1*   **$13.95**
In the Cosmopolitan Magazine for May, 1910, and in the Contemporary Review (London) for April, 1910, I published an article dealing with my experiences in fasting. I have written a great many magazine articles, but never one which attracted so much attention... New Age/Self Help/Health Pages 164

Hebrew Astrology *by Sepharial*   ISBN: *1-59462-308-2*   **$13.45**
In these days of advanced thinking it is a matter of common observation that we have left many of the old landmarks behind and that we are now pressing forward to greater heights and to a wider horizon than that which represented the mind-content of our progenitors... Astrology Pages 144

Thought Vibration or The Law of Attraction in the Thought World   ISBN: *1-59462-127-6*   **$12.95**

by William Walker Atkinson   *Psychology/Religion Pages 144*

Optimism *by Helen Keller*   ISBN: *1-59462-108-X*   **$15.95**
Helen Keller was blind, deaf, and mute since 19 months old, yet famously learned how to overcome these handicaps, communicate with the world, and spread her lectures promoting optimism. An inspiring read for everyone... Biographies/Inspirational Pages 84

Sara Crewe *by Frances Burnett*   ISBN: *1-59462-360-0*   **$9.45**
In the first place, Miss Minchin lived in London. Her home was a large, dull, tall one, in a large, dull square, where all the houses were alike, and all the sparrows were alike, and where all the door-knockers made the same heavy sound... Childrens/Classic Pages 88

The Autobiography of Benjamin Franklin *by Benjamin Franklin*   ISBN: *1-59462-135-7*   **$24.95**
The Autobiography of Benjamin Franklin has probably been more extensively read than any other American historical work, and no other book of its kind has had such ups and downs of fortune. Franklin lived for many years in England, where he was agent... Biographies/History Pages 332

Name	
Email	
Telephone	
Address	
City, State ZIP	

☐ **Credit Card**   ☐ **Check / Money Order**

Credit Card Number	
Expiration Date	
Signature	

Please Mail to: Book Jungle
                      PO Box 2226
                      Champaign, IL 61825
or Fax to: 630-214-0564

ORDERING INFORMATION

web*: www.bookjungle.com*
email*: sales@bookjungle.com*
fax*: 630-214-0564*
mail*: Book Jungle PO Box 2226 Champaign, IL 61825*
or PayPal *to sales@bookjungle.com*

Please contact us for bulk discounts

DIRECT-ORDER TERMS

**20% Discount if You Order
Two or More Books**
Free Domestic Shipping!
Accepted: Master Card, Visa,
Discover, American Express

www.ingramcontent.com/pod-product-compliance
Lightning Source LLC
Chambersburg PA
CBHW080823020726

47501CB00009B/2397